The Pineapple Weekly Journal

PUBLISHED FIFTY TIMES A YEAR

Rampaging Giant Attacks Pineappler

Has the Figg-Newton giant grown too tall?

"Yes," says Alma Lumpholtz. "It's bad for my blood pressure."

Mrs. Lumpholtz was on her way home from Harriet's Beauty Salon at four o'clock yesterday afternoon when the Figg-Newton giant appeared. It made threatening gestures and nearly toppled on her head, forcing her to take refuge in the newly installed telephone booth at the corner of Hemlock and Ash, which the giant then proceeded to shake.

"A person is not safe on the streets anymore," said Mrs. Lumpholtz, who is contributing ten cents to the "Separate the Figg from the Newton" campaign.

NOVELS BY ELLEN RASKIN

Ellen Raskin

Figgs & Phantoms

PUFFIN BOOKS
An Imprint of Penguin Group (USA) Inc.

PUFFIN BOOKS

Published by the Penguin Group

Penguin Young Readers Group, 345 Hudson Street, New York, New York 10014, U.S.A.

Penguin Group (Canada), 90 Eglinton Avenue East, Suite 700, Toronto, Ontario, Canada M4P 2Y3
(a division of Pearson Penguin Canada Inc.)

Penguin Books Ltd, 80 Strand, London WC2R 0RL, England

Penguin Ireland, 25 St Stephen's Green, Dublin 2, Ireland (a division of Penguin Books Ltd)

Penguin Group (Australia), 250 Camberwell Road, Camberwell, Victoria 3124, Australia
(a division of Pearson Australia Group Pty Ltd)

Penguin Books India Pvt Ltd, 11 Community Centre, Panchsheel Park, New Delhi - 110 017, India

Penguin Group (NZ), 67 Apollo Drive, Rosedale, North Shore 0632, New Zealand
(a division of Pearson New Zealand Ltd)

Penguin Books (South Africa) (Pty) Ltd, 24 Sturdee Avenue,
Rosebank, Johannesburg 2196, South Africa

Registered Offices: Penguin Books Ltd, 80 Strand, London WC2R 0RL, England

First published in the United States of America by E. P. Dutton,
a division of NAL Penguin Inc., 1974
Published by Puffin Books, 1989
This edition published simultaneously by Puffin Books and Dutton Children's Books,
divisions of Penguin Young Readers Group, 2011

1 3 5 7 9 10 8 6 4 2

THE LIBRARY OF CONGRESS HAS CATALOGED THE PUFFIN EDITION AS FOLLOWS:
Raskin, Ellen
Figgs & phantoms / by Ellen Raskin.   p.   cm.
Summary: Chronicles the adventure of the unusual Figg family after
they left show business and settle in the town of Pineapple.
ISBN 0-14-032944-7
[1. Family life—Fiction.] I. Title. II. Title: Figgs and phantoms.
PZ7.R1817Fi 1989 [Fic]—dc19 88-29910 CIP AC

Puffin ISBN 978-0-14-241169-8

Printed in the United States of America
Set in Janson

★ ★ ★ ★ ★

CONTENTS

★ ★ ★ ★ ★

★ ★ ★ ★ ★

1. THE FIGG-NEWTON GIANT

★ ★ ★ ★ ★

THE BLACK-CLAD GIANT moved slowly, silently, like a grotesque late-afternoon shadow, past the shops on Hemlock Street. Head erect, shaded eyes unseeing, the monstrous, hovering creature seemed to defy nature as it balanced its teetering bulk on two small feet.

Suddenly the giant stumbled. Its head whipped backward, forward; its flailing arms thrashed the air. The huge, distorted body threatened to break in two as it writhed and swooped, twisting and lurching in ragged circles. At last it jackknifed to a stop atop the telephone booth where Mrs. Lumpholtz had run for cover.

"Figgs!" hissed Mrs. Lumpholtz.

The giant pushed against the booth and straightened to its more than nine feet. A dime clinked into the coin-return slot.

"We're so sorry, Mrs. Lumpholtz," the giant apologized. The muffled voice seemed to come from the fourth button of its tattered cloak.

"You're too old for such childishness, Mr. Florence I. Figg," Mrs. Lumpholtz snarled back at the fourth button. Pocketing the dime, she squeezed out of the booth, shook a fist at the scowl under the wide black hat, and spluttered, "And you're getting too . . . too big, Mona Lisa Newton!"

The scowl deepened. Mona struggled to think of a cutting reply equal to her bruised feelings. Words tumbled around in her head, stumbled and bumped into one another and lay dead, unspoken. Mrs. Lumpholtz huffed off to the office of *The Pineapple Weekly Journal* (published fifty times a year) as Mona watched in dumb anguish.

★ *"Figgs!" the people of Pineapple said. "And that Mona Newton's the worst of the lot. Just look at her balancing up there like Truman the Human Pretzel. She's a Figg, all right, even if she can't tap-dance."*

Mona adjusted her feet on the shoulders of her Uncle Florence and released her grip on the telephone booth. "Ready," she called.

Knees buckling, the Figg-Newton giant staggered on its unsteady way toward Bargain Books.

"You are growing up, Mona," Uncle Florence mumbled. "You are growing up, and I am growing old."

★ ★ ★ ★ ★

Mona dipped her knees and ducked her head as Uncle Florence stepped through the doorway of the bookshop.

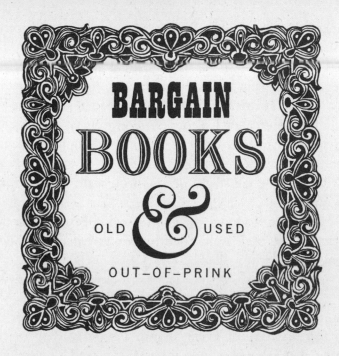

BARGAIN
BOOKS
OLD & USED
OUT—OF—PRINK

The giant paused to adjust to the dim dustiness, then shuffled toward the rear wall, past Ebenezer Bargain perched on a tall stool behind his high desk. The wizened bookseller was bent over a book, thick glasses weighing heavily on his beaked nose.

Mona bit hard on her upper lip, trying to stifle a sneeze as she stared down from the dizzying height at the small bald spot on top of the old man's head. The bald spot reflected the shop's one hanging bulb; and it seemed to Mona that years of sitting in the same position must have burned this desert patch in his thicket of silver hair.

Then Mona sneezed. Jolted, Uncle Florence gripped his niece's ankles firmly as she flapped her arms like a landing goose. The giant reeled giddily, slammed into book bins and stumbled against the shelves. Clutching a bracketed support, Uncle Florence gasped for breath. Mona glanced around furtively.

The bald spot shone as if with a light of its own. Ebenezer Bargain was still bent over his book, avidly reading. He swore softly at the disturbance and turned a page, but he did not look up. The crotchety shopkeeper had no need to look up. His valuable books were secure from all browsers, he thought, safely out of sight and out of reach on the tall stacks on the back wall. On the very top shelf.

Masked in shadows, the giant stood tall before the tall stacks on the back wall. Silently, Mona removed a book from the very top shelf.

★ ★ ★ ★ ★

On the first day of every month Ebenezer Bargain rearranged the books in his shop. He placed slow-selling items in sale bins to make room for newly acquired books and added one or two rare or unusual books to the top-shelf collection, his "retirement investment."

On the second day of every month the Figg-Newton giant appeared.

Three years ago Mona had convinced her Uncle Florence, who was also a bookseller, that if old man Bargain had not yet retired, he never would. He was then ninety-three years old. Besides, she had argued, books should not be hoarded. There were surely some books gathering dust on the top shelf that her uncle's customers would pay dearly to own. Florence reluctantly agreed, on one condition: they would take no more than the number added. So every month Ebenezer Bargain added one or two books to his top shelf, and the next day the Figg-Newton giant removed one or two books from the top shelf. The old shopkeeper never seemed to notice that the length of his "retirement investment" remained the same.

Teetering on her uncle's shoulders, Mona flipped through the worn book to make certain it was the same book she had seen and described to him last month. She found the delicately colored, decorative map, then hastily turned to the title page.

LAS HAZAÑAS FANTÁSTICAS

*Historia de la vida y hechos
del*

Pirata Supuesto

M D C C X *Madrid*

Mona bent her knees and cautiously placed the Spanish book into the upraised hand protruding through two buttons of the shabby cloak. Uncle Florence placed the book on the third shelf from the bottom, and the giant continued its slow progress along the back wall.

Three times more Mona nudged her uncle with her toe, and each time he stopped, allowing her to examine the new addition and commit details to memory. At last the giant reached the end of the row. Mona looked around for the all-clear signal. The shopkeeper's bald spot beamed like a lighthouse in a fog: old man Bargain was still bent over his book. The Figg-Newton giant emerged from the shadows and shuffled out of the shop into the sun.

★ ★ ★ ★ ★
2. ALMOST A MIDGET
★ ★ ★ ★ ★

Hey, Figg-Newton. I sure could use you on my basketball team," Bump Popham shouted as the giant staggered past Benckendorf's Drugs and Sodas (Booths in the Back).

Florence, deep in the folds of the long cloak, was panting too hard to greet the athletic coach.

Mona, too, remained silent, bitterly silent; she teetered on her uncle's shoulders, arms thrashing, cheeks burning with rage. Bump Popham was making fun of them, she thought. Just because they were Figgs, she thought. Just because Uncle Florence was short, she thought. And now Bump Popham will tell everybody his joke, *ha! ha!* And everybody will laugh, *ha! ha!* That's all the people of Pineapple did these days was laugh and gossip about Figgs, she thought. Figgs. Figgs. The funny Figgs. The poor, funny, freaky Figgs.

★ *"Poor Florence Italy Figg,"* the people of Pineapple said. *"Forty-five years old next week and still only four-feet six-inches tall. As if it wasn't bad enough having to go through life with a name like that, he has to be almost a midget. Still, as Figgs go, he's the best of the lot, by far."*

The glum giant flapped around the corner and disappeared into a small shack on Newt Newton's used-car lot. Seconds later a little man scurried out, retracing the giant's steps. He patted his graying hair into place, tugged down his tight vest, hiked his overlong shirt sleeves up over the yellow garters Sister had given him last Christmas, and slipped into the jacket of his once-elegant suit. Then, wincing as he threw back his sore shoulders, Florence Italy Figg stepped into Hemlock Street, proud and dignified, as if to cheat the curious out of a lingering stare.

"Hello, Bump," he said as he passed Benckendorf's Drugs. The coach was still leaning in front of the streamered window display. "No baseball game today?"

"Team's rehearsing for the parade," Bump Popham explained. "Are you going to be in it, Flo?"

"I hope not," Flo replied. "I'm getting a bit old and creaky."

"You're as young as you feel, I always say." The coach reinforced his adage with a mock jab to the little man's ribs. "But you're welcome to ride on the float with me."

"Thanks, Bump," Florence said, "but you know Sister." He continued on his way with a smile that never quite disguised the sadness in his eyes, and entered Bargain's dark shop, where he would spend the rest of the afternoon dickering over the price of a book he had just happened to find on the third shelf.

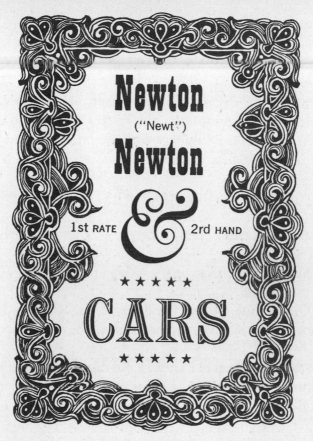

Newton
("Newt")
Newton
&
1st RATE   2rd HAND
★ ★ ★ ★ ★
CARS
★ ★ ★ ★ ★

Giant Day was a busy day for Newton ("Newt") Newton. Strangers driving through Pineapple were so fascinated by the gargantuan creature that they followed it straight into the used-car lot. "Cheap advertising stunt," some said when they realized where the trip had taken them, but a few remained to trade in their cars. Somehow Newt managed to lose money in almost every deal.

Mona emerged from the shack dressed in her usual uniform of a pea jacket, an old shirt, and jeans, as Newt was halfheartedly describing the merits of a Buick convertible to a potential buyer, who kicked a half-inflated tire and frowned.

"Great little car," Mona said in passing. "Tires just need some air."

"That's my daughter," Newt explained proudly.

Mona clumped into Newt's Office (Everybody Welcome), and dialed a familiar telephone number. She had a more important sales pitch to make.

★ ★ ★ ★ ★

"AAAA Universal Travel Bureau," a strained falsetto voice answered.

"May I speak to Romulus Figg, please. This is Ms. Newton calling."

"One minute, please, I will see if Mr. Romulus Figg, proprietor, travel expert, and tour guide extraordinaire is in."

Mona waited out her Uncle Romulus' pretense. Exactly one minute later he replied in his natural baritone.

"Hello, hello, Romulus Figg here."

"Uncle Romulus, I've just found the perfect book for you. Uncle Florence has two or three customers just begging for it, but I wanted you to have first choice."

"How much is it going to set me back this time?"

"Whatever it costs, it will be worth it. I'm sure it's a very rare book. It's by someone named Supuesto, and it has the strangest map. . . ."

"Map of what?"

"Las Hazanas Fantasticas. That's probably Havana. Fantastic Havana," Mona translated, incorrectly.

"Havana is Havana, and Hazanas is Hazanas, except

there is no such place as Hazanas," Romulus (Ask Me Anything) Figg replied. "Never mind, when can I see the book?"

"Tomorrow, I guess, or the next day." Mona's voice faltered. "Tonight is Phoebe night, so Uncle Florence won't be over for dinner."

Romulus softened his tone. "Thanks, Mona, I really would like to take a look at the book. Tell me, how's my favorite niece these days? How's the diet coming?"

Mona slammed the receiver in her uncle's ear. Favorite niece, indeed. She was the only niece he had.

Diet!

Phoebe!

Newt leaned through the office door. "Want to come along on a demonstration ride, Mona? I'll drop you off at home on the way back."

Mona brushed past her father without a word and stamped out of the car lot, fists in her pockets, chin on her chest, propelled by an inner fury.

Phoebe! Why did Uncle Florence have to have a date with Phoebe on Giant Day? Giant Day was her day, hers and Uncle Florence's together. Everyone wanted to spoil it. Bump Popham. Mrs. Lumpholtz. "I should have said: 'Five cents of that is mine, Mrs. Lumpholtz.' I should have shouted: 'Mrs. Lumpholtz, five cents of that dime you stole from the telephone company is mine.'"

★ ★ ★ ★ ★

Tap-tappity-tap-tap. Mona was home.

★ ★ ★ ★ ★

★ *"A crazy lot, those Figgs," the people of Pineapple said. "Not our kind at all. How Newt Newton, the best high school quarterback this town's ever had, could have married the likes of that tap-dancing Sister Figg is more than a person can imagine. Serves him right, his one and only child turning into such a misfit."*

3. TAP-DANCING MOTHER

TAPPING. Resounding, ear-shattering tap-tap-tap-tapping. Mona had grown used to her mother's incessant tap-dancing, but this sounded like a buffalo stampede. Even the front stoop where she was sitting shook as the thundering herd stamped and sang "Take Me Out to the Ballgame."

Shutting her ears, closing her eyes, Mona tried to concentrate on the new additions she had discovered on Bargain's top shelf.

★ *"That Mona Newton is a Figg, all right,"* the people of *Pineapple said. "Looks like a Figg, acts like a Figg. Balances like her uncle Truman the Human Pretzel. Memorizes like Romulus, the Walking Book of Knowledge. Figures like Remus, the Talking Adding Machine. Short, too, like Florence, though she's still growing—both ways. Wouldn't be so bad if she took after her cute mother, but she's going to end up looking like Kadota, and she doesn't even like dogs."*

Deep in thought, Mona was almost trampled by the Pineapple Slicers. Rehearsal over, the high school baseball team bounded through the front door, laughing, punching, clowning. Mona darted around to the side of the house and waited until she heard Fido Figg, boisterous star pitcher, leave. If there was one person Mona truly hated in that hateful town, it was her cousin Fido Figg.

No one's too old or lame to learn

TAP ★★★★ DANCING

&

BATON-TWIRPING

from Pineapple's perennial cheerleader

Sister Figg Newton

"There you are, Mona," Sissie Newton said, tap-dancing toward her daughter with welcoming arms. "Fido was disappointed he didn't see you."

Mona ducked, successfully eluding her mother's kiss, and plopped down into the old couch.

Sissie shrugged off the now-familiar rejection and began tap-dancing the furniture back into place. "Mona, dear, please give me a hand."

Sighing, Mona rose, pushed the sofa to the center of the room, then slumped back into its sagging springs. Noodles, her cat, missed being squashed by a hair. He sprang off the couch and meowed a complaint from under the piano.

"Is anything wrong?" Sissie asked.

"I'm thinking," Mona replied.

"That's nice, dear," her mother said, and tapped off to the kitchen to prepare dinner.

★ *"Those Newtons," the people of Pineapple said, "don't even have carpets like decent folk do. Sister says she can't tap-dance on carpets. If Newt wanted to marry a dancer he should have picked a ballerina. At least a ballerina wouldn't make so much noise."*

"Anybody home?" Newt boomed, bouncing through the front door. "What a day. What a glorious spring day."

"Newt, darling, is that you?" Sissie called from the kitchen. Mona groaned at the silly question; who else would be so disgustingly happy?

Hands behind his back, Newt waited for his wife to make her grand entrance.

"Looky, Looky, Looky, Here Comes Cookie," sang

Sissie, tapping into the living room with a double shuffle. She topped off her performance with a buck and wing and a deep curtsy.

Newt bowed, extended his left hand with a flourish, and presented his wife with a daffodil. "And where's my beautiful Mona?"

Newt tracked the grunt of disgust to the sofa. He bowed again and presented his daughter with a lilac. "And some spring for my little blossom."

Mona took the flower with a limp hand, put it on the coffee table and stroked the cat, who was now lying on her stomach.

"Don't you feel well, princess?" Newt asked.

"She's thinking," Sissie explained, and tapped to the kitchen, the daffodil between her teeth.

★ ★ ★ ★ ★

Mona thought throughout most of dinner, shrugging off questions about school and the book business. Newt finally drew her into the conversation with news of his latest trade: the blue Buick for a raspberry-red Edsel.

"What!" Mona exclaimed.

"Well, I, for one, think it was a wonderful deal," Sissie said. "Raspberry is such a gay color, and we can always use an Edsel in the Founders' Day parade."

"Besides," Newt explained sheepishly to his disapproving daughter, "money isn't everything."

He had used this excuse so often that Mona had a comeback ready. "Money happens to be one of our few compensations in this vale of tears."

"Why, that's very clever, princess," Newt said, impressed with his daughter's quick wit.

"Say that again, Mona, please," Sissie pleaded. "I like the sound of those big words."

"Never mind."

Sissie, unaware of having ruined Mona's insult with her praise, chatted happily about her plans for the Founders' Day parade while her sulking daughter comforted herself with a heaping of mashed potatoes.

★ *"Founders' Day!" the people of Pineapple said. "As if Sister Figg Newton didn't have enough holidays to dance and prance around in, she has to invent Founders' Day. And she wasn't even born here. Wouldn't be so bad if she knew who the real founders were, but the town records were lost in the fire of '08. All anybody knows for sure is that Pineapple wasn't named after pineapples. Pineapples don't grow within three thousand miles of here."*

Fingers extended, Sissie counted off possible origins for the town's name that she had compiled with the help of Rebecca Quigley, the public librarian:

1. Pine-apple, meaning pine cone. (Lots of pines around here.)
2. Pink-apple. (After all, who would want to name a town Crabapple?)
3. Penelope, the name of a founding mother.
4. Pinnacle. (Because of Grubb Hill, altitude 537 feet.)

Newt offered a fifth possibility: the old trading post was won in a pinochle game.

"That's wonderful, sweetheart," Sissie exclaimed. "And we can dress Florence as a one-eyed jack."

Mona protested so violently that her mother changed the costume to the King of Hearts.

"By the way," Newt asked, "where is Flo tonight?"

"He's with Phoebe," Mona replied furiously. She slathered margarine on a slice of bread with such force that it crumbled in her hand.

Newt was utterly confused by his daughter's anger. "What's wrong, princess?" he asked meekly.

"What's wrong?" Mona replied. "What's wrong is that I don't think there is or ever has been a Phoebe. That's what's wrong."

"Don't be silly, Mona," Sissie said. "Of course there's a Phoebe. She's intelligent and kind and loves books. And she's four-feet four-inches tall."

"How do you know?" Mona challenged. "Have you ever seen her?"

"Well, no," Sissie admitted, "but your Uncle Florence described her to me. He's good at describing, you know."

Mona wasn't convinced. "If there is a Phoebe, how come none of us have met her?"

"Gee, princess, Flo is entitled to some privacy," Newt said. "Besides, he's too smart to let Phoebe meet a Figg."

Newt and Sissie laughed, but Mona didn't think it was funny.

4. A BAD PRESS

DOTS FOR EYES, a blob for a nose, a line for a mouth. Mona combed the limp mouse-brown hair that refused to grow longer and studied herself in the bathroom mirror. What should have been small was big; what should have been big was small. She looked even worse than her Uncle Kadota, she thought. Kadota didn't have pimples.

Something worse than her own reflection awaited Mona in the kitchen. Fido was sitting at the breakfast table with her parents, blowing his perpetually runny nose.

"Morning, princess," Newt said cheerfully. "You made the front page of *The Pineapple Weekly Journal*."

Mona read the newspaper her father held before her as she poured dry cereal into her bowl. The Corn Flakes overflowed and sprinkled in her lap.

The Pineapple Weekly Journal

PUBLISHED FIFTY TIMES A YEAR

Rampaging Giant Attacks Pineappler

Has the Figg-Newton giant grown too tall?

"Yes," says Alma Lumpholtz. "It's bad for my blood pressure."

Mrs. Lumpholtz was on her way home from Harriet's Beauty Salon at four o'clock yesterday afternoon when the Figg-Newton giant appeared. It made threatening gestures and nearly toppled on her head, forcing her to take refuge in the newly installed telephone booth at the corner of Hemlock and Ash, which the giant then proceeded to shake.

"A person is not safe on the streets anymore," said Mrs. Lumpholtz, who is contributing ten cents to the "Separate the Figg from the Newton" campaign.

"That's a lie; Mrs. Lumpholtz bumped into us," Mona protested, jumping up from her chair. A shower of Corn Flakes rained on the floor.

"Well, I do worry about your getting hurt, princess," Newt said, placing a comforting arm around Mona's shoulders. "Maybe you are getting too big for that balancing act. You are taller than Florence now, and it's a

long way down if you fall. Besides, Flo hasn't been looking at all well lately."

Mona wrenched out of her father's hug and ran out
of the house, followed by cries of "Mona! Hey, Mona!
Wait!"

Fido caught up with her at the corner. "What in the
world's the matter with you, Mona? That's not the first
bad review a Figg ever got."

"Just leave me alone, Fido Figg. The answer is no."

"No, what? I haven't asked you anything yet." Fido
fumbled for his handkerchief. By the time he had pulled
it out of his pocket and blown his nose Mona was two
blocks away.

"Hey, Mona! Wait!"

Mona didn't wait.

★ ★ ★ ★ ★

"What's wrong with Mona?" Newt asked. "She's so
touchy these days."

Sissie replied with a tap-tappity-crunch-crunch as she
carried the dishes to the sink over the cereal-studded floor.

At one time early in their marriage Newt had studied
Morse code on the chance that Sissie was tapping out
messages to him. Occasionally he picked out something
like "string bean," but the rest was nonsense. At least it
wasn't English.

Today's word was "mousetrap." Newt shrugged and
left for the used-car lot, deciding he would have to talk to
Florence about his moody daughter.

1. FABULOUS FIGGS BUS

FLORENCE no longer lived in Acorn Alley, in the house he had built with his own hands. He had lived there for fifteen years; he had raised his little sister there after their parents had died (shuffled off to Buffalo, as Sissie put it); he had held her wedding there. Then Newt moved in. Then Mona was born. The house was not large enough for four people and a library; either Florence or his books had to go. The books stayed. Mona moved into Florence's bedroom and Florence moved into the Fabulous Figgs bus, permanently parked in Newton ("Newt") Newton's used-car lot.

Newt rapped on the dented door of the derelict bus. He rapped again. "Flo," he called. "Wake up, Flo." Through a window he could see Florence asleep on his cot, smiling a dream smile.

Newt climbed into the bus and gently, then firmly, shook his brother-in-law. Florence opened his eyes and looked around. His smile faded.

"Morning, Flo. I sure envy you your dreams."

Groggy with sleep, Florence sat up slowly, painfully. "Morning, Newt. Did Mona get off to school all right?"

"Hardly," Newt replied. He squeezed into the desk chair opposite the cot and handed Florence a container of coffee. "I'm really worried about Mona, Flo. I can't figure out what's going on in her head. She's so inside herself these days, and so mad at the world. She won't confide in Sissie. Or me. You're the only one she talks to lately."

"I'm afraid she doesn't confide in me either, Newt. We just talk about the book business. Not about books, unfortunately, just the business." Florence sipped the luke-warm coffee and shook his head sadly. "I had hoped to teach her to enjoy books, to love books, but maybe that's something that can't be taught. Books, to Mona, are just things to be bought and sold."

"Well, at least she's interested in something, Flo, thanks to you. Sometimes I think it wasn't such a good idea, her being put ahead in school. Smart as she is, it must be tough being the youngest in her class. And the smallest." Newt immediately regretted his words.

Shoulders slumped, feet dangling over the edge of the cot, Florence agreed. "It can be a problem, being the smallest."

"I'm sorry, Flo. Nothing personal, I mean. . . ." Newt swallowed his clumsy apology and dashed out of the bus on the pretense that a customer had just walked into his office.

Florence was too fond of his brother-in-law to be

offended. "Thanks for the coffee, Newt," he shouted after him. Then, whistling the left-hand piano accompaniment to Schubert's "Who Is Sylvia?", he put on his bathrobe and left the bus. In lighter moments he whistled Gilbert and Sullivan.

One of Florence's dreams had been to become a great pianist. He had traveled too much as a child to take lessons, and when he finally settled down in a house with a piano he discovered that his legs were too short and his hands too small. And now arthritic, he thought. He had also dreamed of becoming a great singer, but his voice was not as gifted as his tapping feet. So the former dancing star, now book dealer, whistled as he crossed the used-car lot.

"Florence I. Figg!" a voice screeched. Florence I. Figg came to an abrupt stop in the middle of the lot. "You'll catch your death of cold running about half-naked, and in bare feet, too."

"Good morning, Mrs. Lumpholtz." Florence pulled his bathrobe tightly around his middle to guard against any indecency, bowed quickly, and trotted off to the shack marked Very Private Office.

★ ★ ★ ★ ★

Properly dressed in his proper suit, Florence left the miniature bathroom and dressing room Newt had built for him and hobbled back to the bus. His knees were bothering him again. His muscles had never been so sore. Absentmindedly rubbing a tender shoulder, he thought of Mona. He, too, was worried about the troubled, lonely Mona.

Suddenly his body was racked by a paroxysm of coughing.

Mona needed him, and there was so little time before he left for Capri.

The words on the side of the bus, once poster-color bright, could barely be read now. Florence flicked a bit of peeling paint off the word "Baby" and limped up the steps.

The bus served both as his home and his office. Figg's Fine Books specialized in colorplate books, issuing catalogues four times a year. Honest in his dealings, loving in his descriptions, Florence had built up a steady list of customers over the years. He used to display choice books in the bus, until the day Newt sold a book-buyer's car by mistake. Now it was strictly a mail-order business.

Las Hazañas Fantásticas lay on the desk. Grimacing with pain, Florence eased himself into the swivel chair, fondly caressed the worn leather binding, and opened the book to the delicately colored map.

Then he smiled his dream smile.

★ ★ ★ ★ ★

"Did you see the dumb story in *The Pineapple Weekly Journal* this morning?" Mona had to repeat her question before Florence looked up from his book, baffled. "Mrs. Lumpholtz is going to ruin everything. What if old man Bargain reads it?"

"Eb Bargain only reads obituaries," her uncle replied seriously. "And I wouldn't worry about Mrs. Lumpholtz. She means well. But why aren't you in school?"

"It's three-thirty," Mona explained, peering over his shoulder. "Is that the map book for Uncle Romulus?"

Florence covered the book with a protective arm. "I don't think we should sell this one to Romulus; the map doesn't appear to be authentic. You remember what happened two years ago."

Two years ago Romulus conducted a tour to Amoscarl Isle. Only after sailing in circles for ten days, threatened with mutiny, did he realize that the island did not exist. Amos Carlisle was the mapmaker's signature.

"But I promised Uncle Romulus he could see the book," Mona complained. It wasn't her fault her tour-guide uncle was stupid enough to chase after nonexistent islands.

Florence comforted her with a "We'll see," and explained that he had not yet catalogued the book. "By the way, what new titles did you find on Bargain's top shelf?"

"Not much," Mona replied, meaning neither colorplate books nor books on the "wanted" lists. "One book is called *The Romance of Sandwich Glass*. Maybe we can interest Sophie Davenport in that one; she collects all kinds of teapots to arrange her flowers in." Mona was always on the lookout for new customers. "And two other books: *Lord Jim* and *Typhoon*."

"Joseph Conrad! Two books by Joseph Conrad!" Florence exclaimed, hoping his enthusiasm was catching. "He's one of my favorite authors; why, I must have read some of his books four or five times. Describe them. They may be first editions."

Eyes closed to help her memory, Mona recited details. "*Lord Jim* . . . a tale . . . London 1900 . . . light green cloth. *Typhoon* . . . New York 1902 . . . dark green binding, decorated cloth, slight tear at top of spine." When she opened her eyes, *Las Hazañas Fantásticas* was no longer on the desk.

"Yes, first editions," Florence said excitedly. "Next month we will take the two Conrads from the top shelf. And, if you'd like, *The Romance of Sandwich Glass*."

★ ★ ★ ★ ★

2. FIDO THE SECOND

★ ★ ★ ★ ★

WHAT IN THE WORLD is the matter with Mona?" Sissie asked. "She tore out of here like a swarm of bees was after her."

Puzzled, Uncle Florence looked over his shoulder. Mona had been right behind him when he entered the house. "Maybe she forgot something at the bus," he suggested, wondering if he had remembered to lock up his special collection.

"No, it's just me," Fido said, pushing the sofa into place. "Mona's been avoiding me like the plague." He stopped to blow his leaky nose. "I've been trying to talk to her for days."

Newt walked in the door, too concerned for his usual ebullient greeting. "What in the world's the matter with Mona? Why is she hiding behind the azalea bush?"

Fido ran out of the front door so fast Newt dropped his tulips.

"For me?" Sissie picked up the flowers and tapped a thank-you dance.

★ *"That Fido's not really a Figg, you know," the people of Pineapple said. "Can tell just by looking at him—so tall and handsome. The best athlete this town's seen since Newt Newton made All-State. Poor kid, he didn't pick that dog-trainer for a father or the dog-catcher for a mother. Imagine Kadota and Gracie Jo adopting a baby to take the place of an old bull terrier. It's a wonder Fido grew up at all, what with walking on all fours until he was six. And eating Ken-L-Ration."*

The door slammed. Mona skidded across the waxed living room floor, stumbled into the kitchen, and fell into her chair at the dinner table.

"Bravo," Sissie applauded. "That's what I call a grand entrance."

Mona bent over her plate and twirled her spaghetti.

"What did Fido want?" Newt asked.

Mona shrugged.

"You mean you still haven't talked to him about whatever it is he wanted to talk to you about?" Newt was incredulous. "I didn't know the Fabulous Figgs had a disappearing act."

"That's not funny, Newt," Mona blurted and slurped up the stray strands of spaghetti.

Florence handed Mona his napkin. "I didn't know you gave classes on Thursday, Sis."

"Must have been a class of elephants," Newt guessed, pointing his fork at the tilted theatrical poster on the wall.

ON STAGE ★ IN PERSON

THE FABULOUS

★ ★ ★ ★ ★ ## FIGGS ★ ★ ★ ★ ★

Toby & Twinkletoes Figg

AND THEIR AMAZING PRODIGIES

★ ★ ★ ★ ★

Truman the Human Pretzel

★ ★ ★ ★ ★

ROMULUS

The Walking Book of Knowledge

& REMUS

The Talking Adding Machine

! ! ! ASK THEM ANYTHING ! ! !

★ ★ ★ ★ ★

KADOTA

& His Nine Performing Kanines

★ ★ ★ ★ ★

★ ★ ★ ★ ★ AND STARRING ★ ★ ★ ★ ★

Baby Flo

★ ★ *Six-year-old Star of Stage & Screen* ★ ★

"The volunteer fire department," Sissie explained. "I'm teaching them a double-time step for Founders' Day." To demonstrate, she tapped to the wall, whistling "The Stars and Stripes Forever," and straightened the framed playbill.

★ *"Figgs!" the people of Pineapple said. "This was a nice, quiet town before those show folk settled here. Had decent celebrations, those days, not like now with Sister Figg Newton making a fool of herself and the volunteer fire department to boot. Not that Sister was ever on the stage herself. Too young. Vaudeville was dead by the time she learned to tap-dance, and the Figgs were never fabulous enough for television. Maybe she wouldn't be tapping her head off now if she had been a real star, like her brother Florence."*

"I hope you're not counting on me to perform on Founders' Day," Florence said.

"Of course I am," his sister replied. "What's a parade without Baby Flo? You're going to be the King of Hearts."

"Really, Mom," Mona complained. "I wish you would stop calling Uncle Florence 'Baby.' He's not six years old anymore."

"For heaven's sake, Mona," Sissie replied. "You know very well that 'Baby' was his stage name, and a very famous one too. Besides, Flo was fifteen when that playbill was made; he just passed for six. And speaking of names, young lady, I wish you would stop calling your father 'Newt.'"

"I don't mind, really," Newt said, trying to avoid another squabble.

"It just isn't right," Sissie insisted. "Besides, she still calls me 'Mom.'"

"Well, I can't very well go around calling my mother 'Sister,' can I?" Mona reasoned. "That's almost as bad as having an uncle named 'Remus.'"

"What's wrong with that?" Sissie asked. "Really, Mona, sometimes I don't understand you at all."

Mona groaned, and once again Uncle Florence came to the rescue.

"Joseph Conrad!" he exclaimed. "Just think, two Joseph Conrads."

★ ★ ★ ★ ★

3. PLOTS AND PLANS

★ ★ ★ ★ ★

MUCH TO MONA'S RELIEF, Fido was not at the breakfast table the next morning. He had taken a cue from his prey and was lurking behind the azalea bush, ready to spring when his cousin left for school.

"Mona, I've got to talk to you," Fido said, grabbing her books as hostages.

"Go ahead and talk," Mona replied haughtily, "but that doesn't mean I'll listen. Just don't let your nose drip on my books."

Fido reached for his handkerchief with his free hand. "You don't even know what I'm going to say."

"Everybody in Pineapple thinks you're so special, Fido Figg II, but they don't know what I know—that you're a disgusting, filthy pig. My answer is no, absolutely and finally no! I will not get you any dirty books."

"That's not what I was going to ask," Fido protested. "Besides, I don't need you to get me pornography; I can get all I want myself."

"See, I told you you had a filthy mind. You're no different from the dogs you live with, Fido Figg."

"The dogs don't read pornography!"

Mona clenched her teeth in anger. "That's all you think about, isn't it, Fido—baseball and sex."

"You're the one who brought it up, not me. Anyhow, just listen a minute, will you? I have a great idea for Uncle Florence's birthday present."

At last Fido had Mona's attention.

The present would be a new paint job for the bus. He would pay for half of the paint and do all the painting if Mona could arrange to keep their uncle away from the bus all day Saturday.

Mona weighed the sharing of her own Uncle Florence against the painting over of the words "The Fabulous Figgs, starring Baby Flo" on the side of the bus.

"All right," she said at last, "but what color?"

Black would look like a hearse, red like a fire wagon, yellow like a school bus, blue like the town bus (it wouldn't do to have people lining up at Uncle Florence's door at rush hour). They agreed on green. Spring green.

Fido had one more suggestion. "Maybe we can get Uncle Truman to letter 'Capri' on the bus door."

"No!" Mona screamed. "No, please no."

Fido was dumfounded by her outburst. "All right, just green. Spring green all over."

Mona turned to hide her tears from an approaching neighbor.

"Good morning, Fido. Hello, Mona. My, aren't you

the lucky one to have such a thoughtful cousin carry your books for you."

"Good morning, Mrs. Lumpholtz," Fido said, shaking her hand.

Mona grabbed her books and ran.

★ ★ ★ ★ ★

Mona thought the school day would never end. She had devised a plan to keep Uncle Florence away from the bus until dark, but she would have to hurry. Saturday was the day after next.

She reread the first (and only) paragraph of her composition, then her mind wandered to Uncle Florence's gasp of delight when he awoke on Sunday, his birthday, and saw the bright, shiny bus. The spring-green bus.

Mona shuddered to think that Fido had wanted that hateful word "Capri" painted on the bus. Uncle Florence wasn't really sick; he just had a virus. He couldn't—he wouldn't go to Capri; not yet, not without her. He couldn't leave her alone in the world with no one but a tap-dancer for a mother and an incompetent used-car dealer for a father.

★ *"Capri," the people of Pineapple said. "Leave it to the Figgs to have some crazy religion of their own. They think their souls will go to a place called Capri when they die. Not the real Capri, but another world all together. Just as well. Who would want to go to heaven if the Figgs were going to be there?"*

The bell rang. Pushing and dodging, Mona ran out of school to the used-car lot.

Newt agreed to buy the paint and be paid back in installments. Leaning into the bus, Mona apologized for not being able to help out today (too much homework) and blew Uncle Florence a kiss.

Fido was waiting on the front porch, blowing his nose. Mona collapsed on the steps next to him, panting for breath.

"What's going on in there?"

"Girl Scouts and their mothers," Fido replied.

"That's going to be a sight not to see," Mona remarked. She had avoided all of her mother's holiday shows for the past three years.

"You don't know what you're missing," Fido said. "The shows are really great fun. Dad's going to let me lead the dogs in the parade this time."

Mona shook her head over the silliness and humiliation of it all, but said nothing. She needed Fido's help if she were going to keep Uncle Florence away from the bus all day Saturday.

"Listen, Fido, I have a plan all worked out. I can tempt Uncle Florence to travel out of town if there is a book collection for sale. Now, old man Bargain subscribes to all the newspapers within two hundred miles so he can read the obituaries and buy up books from dead collectors' relatives. All I have to do is read the obituaries before Bargain does, then make an appointment for Uncle Florence to look at the books."

"How can you get those papers if Mr. Bargain is the only one in town who subscribes to them?"

"You, Fido Figg, are going to steal them!"

"I will not. Honestly, Mona, for someone who hates dirty books. . . ."

"Old man Bargain swears at me, so it's all right."

"It's not all right. If you want to steal them, go ahead; but not me. And how is Uncle Florence going to travel two hundred miles? He doesn't drive, and your folks work Saturdays."

"You'll have to ask your father to drive us."

"Let's get this straight, Mona," Fido said after a long sniff. "I'll paint the bus; I'll pay for half the paint, but the rest is up to you. Good-bye, I'm late for practice."

4. THE POTATO DANCE

How DID your homework go?" Florence asked at the dinner table.

"Terrible," Mona replied, remembering that her composition was overdue. If her plan kept to schedule, she could return to school in time to hand it in, but she had to write it first. "Just terrible."

"That's not like you, princess," Newt said as Sissie carried in a flat cake, tapping and singing "School Days." "You're always so good in school. Not like us, huh, Sis?" Newt chuckled over sweet memories.

"Being good in school isn't everything, Mona," Sissie said. "I wish you'd let me teach you baton-twirling. Or at least some of the cheers."

"Your mom was the best cheerleader Pineapple High ever had," Newt said proudly.

Sister demonstrated her favorite. "With an N. With an E. With a W, T. Newwwwwwwt!"

Unimpressed, Mona left the table and returned with her notebook.

"Why don't you read your composition out loud. Perhaps we can help you," Uncle Florence said, as she had expected.

"The assignment is to describe an imaginary person in five hundred words," Mona explained, then read what she had written:

> "His name was Holtzlump. Conrad Q. Holtzlump, to be exact. The people of Winston-Salem wondered what the Q. stood for. They knew so little about this strange man, who had a nose like a potato and moved like a trombone."

"Me too," Sissie said approvingly. "What does the Q. stand for, I wonder. And how did you ever think up a name like Holtzlump?"

"I'm more concerned with Winston-Salem," Newt said. "You haven't taken up smoking, have you?"

Mona's answer was a wilting glare.

"That's quite good, Mona," Florence said. "Go on."

"That's all I have," Mona confessed. "I can't figure out what kind of a person moves like a trombone."

"Then why did you write it?" Newt asked.

"I like the way it sounds," Mona replied. "Sort of intriguing."

"Your Uncle Truman looks something like a trombone when he's doing his human-pretzel act," Sissie said.

Newt corrected her. "You're thinking of a French horn."

"Well, change it to French horn and write about Truman," Sissie suggested.

"It's supposed to be an imaginary person," Mona replied impatiently. "Besides, who wants to write five hundred words about a double-jointed idiot who bites his toenails?"

"Mona Lisa Newton, what a thing to say about your Uncle Truman!" Sissie scolded.

"Well, it's just what all the people of Pineapple say about him," Mona replied calmly.

"What people?" Newt was aghast. "I don't know anyone who'd say such a thing."

"Never mind." Mona couldn't explain how she knew what everybody said. She just knew.

Worry creased Uncle Florence's face. "Let's get back to your composition. As you say, it is supposed to be an imaginary character."

"I know!" Sissie exclaimed. "Just turn it around, Mona. Make him have a nose like a trombone and move like a potato."

"Move like a potato!" Newt howled.

Sissie giggled uncontrollably. Uncle Florence smiled broadly. Someone repeated "potato" and all three roared with contagious laughter.

Then four.

"Look," Newt gasped, pointing at his daughter. "Look, Mona's laughing!"

Mona stopped laughing.

The others stopped laughing, cleared their throats, and returned to the business at hand.

"I have an idea," Florence said. "Your paragraph is too good to waste. Why don't you put it aside and start again with something you do know? Describe the Figg-Newton giant."

Mona argued that the giant wasn't imaginary, but her uncle explained that although they were each half of the giant, the giant itself was not real.

Mona wasn't sure, but the giant would be simple enough for her to describe: its clothes (which she had sewn), its face (Kadota plus pimples), its arm movements (like a windmill, like a bird).

"Thanks, Uncle Florence." Mona wrapped her arms around her uncle and planted a big kiss on his cheek. Then, turning her back on her parents, she clumped up the stairs to her room.

Newt and Sissie stared sadly after their daughter, stung by the deliberate rejection. At last Sissie rose from the table.

"Moved like a potato," she said, trying to sound cheerful.

Newt forced a loud laugh at Sissie's attempt to imitate a potato dancing. "Hey, Sissie, that's good. That's really very good." His voice broke.

Mona, Mona, Uncle Florence thought. Perhaps it's all for the best that I go to Capri.

★ ★ ★ ★ ★

1. THE THIEF

★ ★ ★ ★ ★

STOP THAT MAN! Stop him!"

Newt stopped jogging and looked around. "Who, me?" Ebenezer Bargain was pointing a spidery finger at him.

"Shame on you, Newton Newton," Mrs. Lumpholtz snapped. "Stealing an old man's mail."

"What are you talking about, Alma? I didn't steal any mail." Newt vindicated himself by opening the burlap bag he had been carrying over his shoulder for the inspection of the crowd. "Just car paint, see? And here's the receipt."

The commotion on Hemlock Street came at a propitious time for Mona, who was hurriedly shuffling through Bargain's mail behind a trash can in the alley. There were no obituaries of book collectors in the newspapers, but she made a more fortunate discovery.

Mrs. Lumpholtz was now accusing Flabby Benckendorf of the theft. The druggist was proclaiming his innocence, and a third voice (a voice remarkably like Uncle Florence's) was appealing to all parties for reason.

Mona stuffed a catalogue in her jacket pocket, opened the back window of the shop, and tossed the rest of the mail and papers onto the top of Ebenezer Bargain's high desk. Her timing was perfect. When she reached the corner the blue town bus was waiting with open doors.

Slumped in a rear seat, Mona studied Saturday's auction catalogue to the end of the line. She then walked the two blocks to the kennels.

"Kadota, go see what's disturbing the dogs." Gracie Jo had her hands full bathing three mongrels in the kitchen sink.

"Down, Mutt; down, Jeff; come here, Boy." Kadota dispersed the dogs one by one until he found Mona at the bottom of the pack. "Everything's all right, Gracie Jo," he called, "it's only Mona, smelling of her cat."

★ *"Dogs!" the people of Pineapple said. "Funny how they've always taken to Gracie Jo. And not only dogs. Once when the circus came to town two elephants and three white horses followed her all the way home. Small wonder she fell in love with that Figg of an animal-trainer. Some doctor he is, with his mail-order degree. Every animal Kadota treats ends up shaking hands. That's all right for dogs, but who wants to shake hands with a cow?"*

The honorary dog-catcher appeared at the screen door carrying the wet pets. "You okay, Mona? Why aren't you in school?"

"I'm just fine, Auntie Gracie Jo," Mona said, picking herself up. "I hope I didn't frighten the animals."

Mona, the model of politeness, ingratiated herself by shaking hands with the yelping dogs. Trying to ignore the rooster that had lighted on her head and the Dalmatian nudging her in the rear, she pleaded her cause. "Fido and I have a plan for Uncle Florence's birthday, and we need your help."

"Fido" was the magic word. Not only did Kadota agree to her requests; he even drove her back to the used-car lot.

★ ★ ★ ★ ★

Mona brushed off the telltale dog hairs, took a deep breath, and prayed that some of the family show-business blood would course through her veins.

"Uncle Florence, look what I've found," she shouted as she leaped up the steps of the Fabulous Figgs bus waving the catalogue.

"What's all the excitement?" Florence asked, surprised by her rare exuberance. Mona shoved the open catalogue into his gnarled hands.

Sale 924. Saturday, at 10 A.M.   12

---

34 [CLEMENS, SAMUEL L.]. Adventures of Huckleberry Finn. New York, 1885.

4to. FIRST AMERICAN EDITION, early issue with "was" for "saw" p. 57, line 23; frontispiece in first state. Original cloth, some wear near top of spine. BAL 2415.

35 COLERIDGE, S. T. The Rime of the Ancient Mariner. London, Ballantyne Press, 1899.

12mo. Woodcut initials on opening page. Green morocco, inlaid and gilt design on upper cover, t.e.g., uncut, by Riviere.

36 CONRAD, JOSEPH. The Secret Agent. A simple tale. London, 1907.

FIRST EDITION. 12mo, original red cloth, with the 40 p. of ads at end dated "September, 1907". Keating 73.

37 CONRAD, JOSEPH. Youth. A narrative and two other stories. Edinburgh and London, 1902.

FIRST EDITION. 12mo, original pale green cloth. With the 32 p. ads dated "10/02". Contains "Heart of Darkness". Keating 34.

"Where did this come from?" The only catalogues Florence received were for sales of colorplate books, but he was soon studying these listings with intense fascination.

"Two Conrads, first editions," he remarked. "And 'Heart of Darkness' is one of my favorite stories."

"Can we go, Uncle Florence? Please?"

"Go where?"

"To the auction, tomorrow, in Middletown?"

"Go all the way to Middletown? How? I can phone in a bid; I don't have to attend the sale."

Mona looked out of the bus window expectantly. "But it's better to be there, if you want a good price. Besides, I've never ever been to an auction." Mona was playing her part well, but it wasn't enough. Florence remained unconvinced.

She changed her tack. "I was hoping we could start a Conrad collection, what with these two books and the two on Bargain's top shelf. I really want to *read* the books, all of them; and it would be so much nicer to read them in the first editions like you did."

Florence laughed. "I'm not that old. But if you want to read the Conrads, if you really want to read them, well, maybe. . . ."

"Yes, really, really," Mona promised. Her plea was interrupted by the expected knock on the bus door.

"Anybody want to buy a dog?"

Kadota squeezed into the bus and plopped down, overlapping two seats, a mangy mutt cradled in his arms. Its coat was so matted and dusty that Mona thought it might be a large rat, but she reached over and shook its paw anyway.

Florence looked puzzled; his brother seldom visited the bus.

"Just passing by," Kadota explained. "Had to look in on Sophie Davenport's goat. Terrible case of indigestion. The poor nanny ate two teapots; the Chelsea wasn't so bad, but the pewter nearly did the critter in."

Mona was impressed with Kadota's wild fib.

"By the way," he continued, "I'm driving to Middletown tomorrow; got a cow there that's ready to drop. Want to come along for the ride, Flo? You too, Mona."

"What an amazing coincidence," Mona exclaimed, clapping her hands in feigned surprise. She was overplaying her role, but she didn't have the stage experience Kadota had. "We were just talking about spending the day in Middletown, weren't we, Uncle Florence?"

"Well, as a matter-of-fact," Florence began, but his brother had already risen and was heading for the door, the mongrel asleep in his arms.

"I'll pick you up tomorrow morning in Acorn Alley. We can talk about it some more at the twins'. It's Capri night, you know."

Mona had forgotten, but she didn't grumble her usual protest. Her plan was working too well to complain about the silly family ritual.

★ ★ ★ ★ ★

2. CAPRIFICATION

★ ★ ★ ★ ★

HAVE YOU GOT great-grandfather's diary, Flo?" Sissie asked as she bounced into the front seat of the Edsel. Caprification was a ceremony, and Sissie took charge of all ceremonies.

"Right here," Florence said, patting the worn diary on his lap.

Sissie turned toward the back seat to make sure.

Mona climbed in next to her uncle and slammed the door hard. "Let's go," she said, impatient to get the evening over with.

Newt started the car. It spluttered and bucked, and at last they were on their way.

"The strangest thing happened to me today," he said. "I was jogging down Hemlock with a sack of pai. . . ."

Mona cleared her throat loudly.

". . . a sack of paper plates," he corrected himself.

"Paper plates?" Sissie mused aloud. "Oh, I know, you're going to string them up around the lot to keep the birds from dirtying the cars."

There was a moment's silence while Newt, Mona, and Florence considered the function of car-lot decorations. Sissie's idea did seem strangely plausible.

"Anyway," Newt went on, "would you believe that somebody stole Ebenezer Bargain's mail?"

"Who would do such an awful thing to that sweet old man?" Sissie asked.

Mona shrugged in wide-eyed innocence and surprise.

"It was just a mistake," Florence said. "Old Eb is getting absentminded; the mail was on his desk all along."

"How did you know that?" Mona asked, now really surprised. She had thought her uncle dealt with Bargain only on Giant Days.

Florence appeared uncomfortable with the question. "I can't remember who told me. By the way, was your Figg-Newton giant composition a success in school?"

Mona went pale. She had completely forgotten about her finished composition. She had taken it with her when she had left the house in the morning; she had returned with only the auction catalogue. Over and over again, Mona retraced the day's activities, but to no avail. There was only one place it could be. She had thrown her composition, along with the mail and newspapers, onto the top of old man Bargain's desk!

"Are you all right, Mona?" Florence felt her forehead for a fever. Mona nodded unconvincingly.

"Maybe I'm catching your virus," she said.

"Oh, by the way, Flo," Newt said into the rearview

mirror, "Alma Lumpholtz came by the lot with a package for you. She wouldn't leave it; said she wanted to give it to you in person."

"It's probably a bomb," Mona said. Newt and Sissie laughed, but she had not meant to be clever.

"Okay, gang, everybody out," Newt said cheerfully as the car suddenly stalled ten blocks from the house of the three Figgs. "Must be the spark plugs."

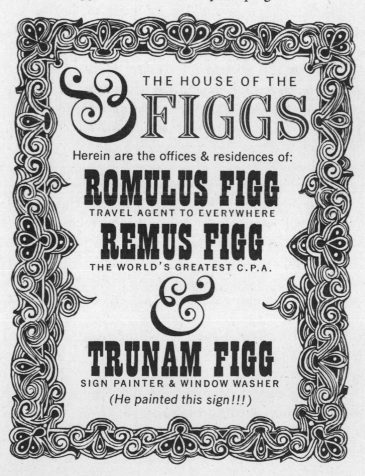

THE HOUSE OF THE
FIGGS
Herein are the offices & residences of:
ROMULUS FIGG
TRAVEL AGENT TO EVERYWHERE
REMUS FIGG
THE WORLD'S GREATEST C.P.A.
&
TRUNAM FIGG
SIGN PAINTER & WINDOW WASHER
(He painted this sign!!!)

Truman greeted the latecomers at the door of the rambling house.

"Got stuck with another lemon, Newt?"

The greeting had been repeated so often over the years it seemed to be part of the ritual.

★ *"That Truman Figg!" the people of Pineapple said. "He's not a double-jointed idiot; he's a triple-jointed idiot. No place too high or snug he can't get to, but he just might paint your windows and wash your signs. Once at Sophie and Doc Davenports' he signed his name on all the windows and painted the washer. He may be a real fancy letterer, but what can Flabby Benckendorf do with a ten-foot sign that reads 'Benckendrug's Dorfs'? There ought to be a law against naming idiots after presidents of the U.S.A."*

The Figg troupe, minus the Kanines, was gathered and waiting in the parlor. Fido winked at Mona, who nodded, indicating all was in order for tomorrow's bus-painting.

> " 'Twas on the Isle of Capri
>   That I met her,
>   'Neath the shade
>   Of an old apple tree. . . ."

Singing and tapping, Sissie entered the room and bowed to imagined applause.

"Everybody ready?" she asked.

Ignoring Remus' remark that they had been ready for half an hour, she directed the congregation into a circle in the middle of the floor. "Now, all sit down," she commanded. "Come on, Mona."

Draped in an easy chair, Mona glumly refused to participate.

"I'll just watch."

"Don't be such a pill, Mona," Fido said. He crossed his feet and lowered himself into the lotus position without using his hands. He was blowing his nose.

Romulus and Remus flopped down together, hand in hand.

Florence sat down almost imperceptibly, having the least way to go. His gasp of surprised pain was drowned out by the loud grunt Kadota emitted as he squatted and bounced on the carpet.

His wife, Gracie Jo, family outsider, knelt down beside him on a cushion.

Newt, always confused about which leg folded over which, was arranged by Sissie.

"Leave room for Truman," she ordered. The floor-sitters sidled, rocked, and knocked into one another as they moved in both directions to make space for the missing brother.

"Here I come," Truman shouted, cartwheeling down the hall. He bounded into the room with two handsprings, leaped up into a one-and-a-half twist, and landed cross-legged on the floor between the twins. He was greeted with shouts and applause.

Caprification was about to begin.

★ ★ ★ ★ ★

The believers closed their eyes. Florence, the eldest, smiled gratefully at the unbelievers, then reverently opened the old diary and read:

I, Jonathan Figg, am a simple farmer.

For 75 years I have grown sweet figs and for 75 years I, Figg, have wondered about figs.

My fig trees make sweet figs because they are pollinated by wasps from the wild fig tree — the CAPRIFIG.

Each year I hang caprifig branches in my sweet fig trees. I watch the caprifig wasps hatch. They dust my blossoms with pollen —and then they die!

Only the wasps that return to the caprifig live.

Now I understand the figs, for I have had a vision. Like the wasp that returns to the caprifig tree, my soul will return whence it came.

My vision:

It was night. I was lost. Then I saw the tree that grows wild and free welcoming me with open arms.

It whispered a name:

"CAPRI."

"Capri!" the Figg family shouted in unison. Florence handed the diary to the next eldest brother, and Kadota read:

———————

I, Noah Figg, son of Jonathan, am a teacher. I believe in the beliefs of my wise father, but this I add:

Not all are blessed with true vision. Some must spend a lifetime searching, building dream upon dream.

The wild, free tree is only the key to the perfect dream.

There are many wasps; there are many trees — each must find his own Capri.

———————

"Capri!" everyone shouted. Now the book should have passed to the next eldest, but no one knew which twin was born first. Together Romulus and Remus recited their father's entry from memory:

---

*I, Toby Figg, son of Noah, am a dancer and showman. I have written these words to the tune of "Battle Hymn of the Republic."
Everybody sing!*

"Mine eyes have seen the glory
　of a tree so wild and free,
That is standing on an island
　that's surrounded by the sea;
Whatsoever, howsoever,
　wheresoever it may be,
All Figgs go to Capri.
　　Glory, glory hallelujah,
　　Glory, glory hallelujah,
　　Glory, glory hallelujah,
　　All Figgs go to Capri."

"Capri!" Truman fell forward onto his palms, stood on his head, somersaulted into the air, and landed squarely on his feet.

The Rite of Caprification was over.

"Somebody give me a hand," Kadota pleaded. Newt and Fido tugged the grunting veterinarian to his feet as, one by one, the members of the family rose from the floor and stretched their cramped muscles. The skeptics went to the kitchen to prepare refreshments, leaving the believers to debate the whereabouts of Capri.

Sissie and Newt were not tempted by the unworldly kingdom. "We like it right here with the sweet fruit," they always said. Kadota and Gracie Jo were also unbelievers, ever since Romulus, returning from a disastrous dogsled trek through Lapland, told them that no Kanines were allowed in anyone's Capri.

Mona remained in the parlor. Although she deeply resented the clannish heresy that set the Figgs apart from the people of Pineapple, she didn't want to miss a word Uncle Florence might have to say. Besides, she was holding down the most comfortable chair in the house.

★ ★ ★ ★ ★

Romulus began the debate by announcing that he was certain of finding Capri on his forthcoming trip to Niagara Falls. His brothers scoffed.

Of course millions of people had been there already, he conceded, but they had not looked where he was going to look: under the falls.

Fido laughed out loud, picturing the faces of the honeymooners when Romulus led them under the falls.

He was banished to the kitchen to join the other doubting Thomases.

"Places, bah," said Remus, who believed Capri lay in numbers. He had spent the past five years dividing the number 1. "Once I get to zero, I'll be in Capri."

Again the brothers scoffed. He could divide 1 an infinite number of times, but it would still be impossible to reach zero.

"Of course it's impossible—here," he explained. "That's why, when I reach zero, I'll know that I'm in Capri. Romulus wouldn't even recognize Capri if he found it."

The twins glared at each other.

★ *"Capri," the people of Pineapple said. "Why don't those Ask Me Anything twins go already and leave us in peace? Poor Alma Lumpholtz went on one of Romulus' South American tours and spent the whole two weeks hacking her way through the jungle. Only folks she met were some naked natives who didn't even speak English. Not that Remus can speak English, not when he's excited. Ran up and down Hemlock once, screaming 6-9-18-5, 6-9-18-5. By the time Harriet Kluttz figured out that the numbers stood for letters of the alphabet, her beauty parlor had burned to the ground."*

Now Florence spoke. Mona listened intently.

"Books. All man has ever known or dreamed of can be found in books," he said. Then he doubled over, coughing and choking. He waved off Truman's offer of a slap on the back.

"I want to go to Capri with you," Mona said, alarmed.

Florence didn't answer. He sat breathless and spent, tears streaming down his cheeks.

"Please, please take me with you, Uncle Florence," Mona cried.

"Come on, princess," Newt said, returning with a tray of cookies. "You know it's not for real."

"And just what is that supposed to mean, Newton Newton?" Truman Figg spluttered. "Just because you aren't looking doesn't mean it's not there. Why, I myself am on the verge of finding Capri. Ever hear of a Moebius band? Take a strip of paper, twist it once and stick the ends together, and what do you have? One side that goes on forever. Infinity. All I have to do is twist my body into a Moebius band and I'll be in Capri. I've just about worked it out, except for one elbow."

"Show me, Uncle Truman," Fido begged, carrying in a pitcher of lemonade.

"Not tonight, Fido," Truman replied. "I'm not quite ready for Capri. I still have to finish painting a sign. It's going to read: HARRIET KLUTTZ, Hair Sets & Cuts. Only $3.95 for a beautiful you (including shampoo)."

★ ★ ★ ★ ★

3. GOING, GOING...

★ ★ ★ ★ ★

UNCLE FLORENCE isn't here yet," Mona announced when Kadota drove up to the Acorn Alley house the next morning.

"Where is he?" Kadota asked. "I just dropped Fido off at the car lot and I didn't see him there."

"Oh, no," Mona wailed, leaping into the car. "Fido will spoil everything. Uncle Florence is probably still asleep in the bus. Hurry."

Kadota screeched into the lot as Florence was scampering out of his Very Private Office.

"Sorry, I overslept," he apologized, settling into the front seat. "Good thing you sent Fido to wake me. I thought it was one of your dogs scratching at the bus until I looked out the window. I can't imagine why he ran away when he saw me."

Kadota backed the car out of the lot so swiftly he nearly ran down a woman with a package the size of a shoebox under her arm.

"Figgs!" hissed Mrs. Lumpholtz.

★ ★ ★ ★ ★

Florence spent the long drive explaining the difficulties of completing a Joseph Conrad collection to Mona. "Many of the first editions are still easy enough to find. Even his first book, *Almayer's Folly*, is obtainable, though it is expensive. But the true 1913 edition of *Chance* is rare, very rare."

"Why do you need first editions when you can read a book in paperback?" Kadota asked.

"Why do you collect dogs?" Mona replied. Kadota remained silent for the rest of the trip, trying to think of an answer.

Florence continued. "The impossible book to find is the original *The Nigger of the Narcissus*."

Mona gasped.

"The British printed only seven, for copyright purposes. The Americans then published what is now considered the first edition, under the title *Children of the Sea*."

"That's much better," Mona said.

"I don't agree," Florence replied, "but read the book, even in paperback if you have to; then decide for yourself." (Read, Mona, read, he thought to himself. Find friends in books when I am gone.)

"Here we are," Kadota announced. "And if my eyes don't deceive me, the sign is another one of Truman Figg's misspelled masterpieces."

A'ction

RARE BOOKS

&

Liter-RARE-y
PROPERTIES

★ ★ ★ ★ ★

Yours for the Bidding

There was still time to examine the books before the sale began. The Conrads were in fine condition. Mona counted the pages of advertisements at the back of the books to make certain the first editions were complete.

"Look at this, Mona." Florence was studying a color-plate book of butterflies. "See how the colors change subtly from lavender to purple to violet?"

Mona glanced hastily at the engraving, then surveyed the shelves of books to be auctioned. "Can we bid on other books if they are good buys?"

Florence sighed. "Let's just concentrate on the Conrads, and you can do the bidding."

Delighted, Mona rushed to the front row to save two seats. She wanted to be sure of being seen by the auctioneer.

★ ★ ★ ★ ★

"Number 34," the auctioneer called out. "Clemens. *Adventures of Huckleberry Finn*. Who'll start the bidding at a hundred dollars? I have a hundred. One-ten. One-twenty. . . ."

Mona had been twisting around to locate bidders on the earlier lots; now she sat forward, biting her lips, eyes fixed on the auctioneer, afraid of missing her opportunity.

"Sold, at one hundred and seventy-five dollars to the gentleman in the third row."

One more number to go.

"Number 35. Coleridge. *The Rime of the Ancient Mariner*. I have a bid for twenty-five. Thirty, thirty-five. Fifty. Do I hear fifty-five? Sold, at fifty dollars, to the lady standing in the rear.

"Number 36. Conrad. *The Secret Agent*. I have a bid of twenty-five. Thirty in the fifth row, forty in the rear, forty-five, fifty, sixty dollars is bid by the gentleman in the seventh row, seventy in the rear. Do I hear seventy-five?"

Mona's mouth was too dry to speak. Florence, arms folded, calmly waited for her to enter the bidding.

"Going at seventy, going, going. . . ."

"Seventy-five," Mona gasped, waving her catalogue in the air. The auctioneer looked at Florence, who nodded his approval.

"I have a bid of seventy-five dollars in the first row. Anyone say eighty?"

The seconds passed like hours as the auctioneer scanned the silent audience.

"Sold at seventy-five dollars to the young lady."

An auction-room assistant approached Florence for a deposit, blocking Mona's view.

"Number 74. Conrad. *Youth*. I have forty dollars, anyone say forty-five?"

Mona stood on her chair to see the auctioneer. "Forty-five," she called.

"Fifty in the rear." The auctioneer looked at Mona, who nodded. "Fifty-five in the first row, sixty in the rear." Again Mona nodded. "Sixty-five in the first row. Anyone say seventy? Sold again to the young lady in the first row."

Mona breathed a deep sigh and collapsed back into her seat. Her heart was pounding at a furious rate.

"Good job," Uncle Florence whispered, and patted her moist hand.

"Number 38," the auctioneer called. Mona and her uncle sat back and enjoyed the rest of the auction, munching on sandwiches Sissie had packed for them.

The last lot was sold at four o'clock. Impatiently, Mona waited in line, money in hand, and was disappointed to be handed wrapped books. She had wanted to look through her purchases once more, but Kadota was honking his horn at the curb.

Kadota spent the return drive explaining why he collected dogs. It was dark when they arrived in Pineapple; it was night when Uncle Florence entered his bus.

★ ★ ★ ★ ★

4. GONE!

★ ★ ★ ★ ★

THE SPRING-GREEN BUS glistened in the Sunday morning sun. "He's still asleep," Newt whispered, peeking into the window.

Quietly, Sissie opened the bus door and, finger to her lips, led her family up the steps.

Mona, smiling in anticipation of Uncle Florence's surprise, tiptoed to the cot and awaited her mother's signal to begin singing.

> "Happy Birthday to you,
> Happy Birthday to you,
> Happy. . ."

"Wake up, Flo," Newt shouted, shaking the little man. "Wake up, Baby," Sissie cried. "Wake up, wake up!" Mona screamed.

The Pineapple Weekly Journal

PUBLISHED FIFTY TIMES A YEAR

Florence Figg Dead

The curtain has fallen on one of Pineapple's most picturesque and respected citizens. Sunday morning Florence Italy Figg, forty-five years old that day, was found dead in his green (?!) bus.

Florence Figg was born to the theatrical team of Toby and Twinkletoes Figg following their matinee performance at the Riverside Theater in Milwaukee. He was named after the great showman Florenz Ziegfeld. When old enough to realize that his parents couldn't spell, Florence adopted the middle name of Italy in tribute to that great center of art and learning.

Florence made his stage debut at the age of two. His fame spread quickly, and by the time he was six his name was in lights. Due to his short stature, he was billed for the next ten years as "Baby Flo, the six-year-old tap dancing wonder." The highlight of his career came when he starred opposite Judy Garland in the motion picture *The Wizard of Oz*. Florence Figg played a Munchkin.

As the Figg family grew, the act was expanded to include his prodigious brothers. "The Fabulous Figgs" became an entire show of their own, and when vaudeville declined they traveled across the country in their bus (now parked in Newton ["Newt"] Newton's used-car lot), performing in carnivals and local extravaganzas.

The Figg family settled in Pineapple, thanks to three

cont. page 3 column 2

cont. from page 1

simultaneous flat tires. Florence went on to become a highly respected dealer in rare colorplate books.

He has left the book business to his niece, Mona Newton, his house in Acorn Alley to his sister, Sister Figg Newton, and the bus to Newton Newton. Also surviving are his four brothers: Kadota, Romulus, Remus, and Truman the Human Pretzel.

Florence Italy Figg will be sorely missed by friends and book collectors alike. He is mourned by all the people of Pineapple, who heartily applauded his dancing at Fourth of July pageants.

Florence Figg has taken his last bow.

1. MONA MOURNS

THE FIGGS WEPT. The Newtons wept. They wept for things they had said and done; they wept for things unsaid, undone. They wept, each in his own way, privately and in one another's arms. Kadota's dogs howled every night for a week, then were silent. And the Figgs and the Newtons ran out of tears.

"Florence is in Capri," they agreed, and resumed their living, filling their loss with memories.

Not Mona. Her tears were still unshed.

Newt stared out of his office window at the spring-green bus, remembering Flo, worrying about Mona. Mona had gone to bed the day Florence died, and she was still there, jealously guarding her loneliness. She barely ate, and she hardly spoke. She rejected everyone as she felt Florence had rejected her. She even rejected her cat, Noodles, who finally ran away in wounded pride.

Newt was startled out of his concern by a figure emerging from the bus's shadow. He called out, but Fido ran off when he heard his name.

★ ★ ★ ★ ★

Sissie shook her head dejectedly when Newt walked in the door. The furniture was in place; the playbills hung plumb. His wife had not given a dancing lesson since Florence's death for fear of disturbing Mona. She had even put Band-Aids over her metal taps.

Newt tiptoed up the stairs, followed by the even quieter Sissie. He had brought Mona flowers for a week until he had denuded Mrs. Davenport's garden. He had brought candy, a weaving set, bookends. Now he carried a hatbox. Newt rapped lightly on the bedroom door and waited for the response he knew would not come. He looked forlornly at Sissie.

"Your father's home, Mona," she announced cheerfully as she opened the door.

Mona turned her face to the wall.

"I brought you a present, princess," Newt said, placing a box at the foot of the bed.

"My, my, I wonder what it could be," Sissie said, lifting the lid.

Mona sat up slowly, her face pale and impassive. A cat peered out of the box and blinked at her. It was Noodles.

"Gracie Jo found him, and. . . ."

Mona sank down into bed and buried her face in the pillow. Noodles sprang out of the box, ran out of the room and out of the friendless house.

Unexpectedly, Mona spoke.

"Was Phoebe at the funeral?" she asked in a flat voice.

Sissie and Newt stared at each other. The funeral had taken place weeks ago, and they had been too enveloped in their own grief at the time to have noticed who was present.

"There were so many people there, princess," Newt said hesitantly. "Your Uncle Florence was a much-loved man."

"Was Phoebe there?" Mona repeated.

"We don't know, honey," Sissie replied. "It would have been hard to see Phoebe; she's only four-feet four-inches tall, you know."

Mona pulled the blanket over her head.

Newt tried to reach his daughter again. He spoke of the book business and the heap of unanswered mail. He told her about his latest trade, a black Cadillac for a sky-blue Studebaker. Mona didn't even groan.

Shoulders hunched, Newt left the room.

"Listen to me, Mona," Sissie said. "It's time you came out of your funk and realized there are other people in this world with feelings. I want to see you downstairs at dinner in ten minutes, do you hear?" Sissie tore the tapes off her taps and danced noisily down the stairs, hoping a new approach would have some effect.

It didn't. Mona remained in bed, wrapped in grief and self-pity, for another week.

★ ★ ★ ★ ★

It was neither gifts nor threats that roused Mona from her bed; it was Fido. Newt found him stalking the bus again and convinced him to speak to Mona.

"Maybe if she talks to someone close to her own age," he suggested, noticing that Fido looked almost as gloomy as his gloomy daughter.

Fido no longer smiled; he no longer laughed. He didn't even leer. Even Mona noticed his hangdog expression. She sat up in bed and spoke to him.

"You're a fink, Fido Figg," she said. "I know they made you come to talk to me, but it won't do any good, so you can just go back to your ball game."

"I quit the team," Fido said, blowing his nose hard and loud. "I wanted to talk to you about Uncle Florence. About how he died."

"Uncle Florence didn't die," Mona replied angrily. What right did Fido have to be sad, she thought bitterly. She was her uncle's favorite.

"He's dead," Fido insisted. Unable to control a sob, he turned and ran down the stairs.

"He's not dead," Mona shouted after him. "He's in Capri. Uncle Florence is in Capri, and I'm going to find him."

"I'm going to find him," Mona repeated, listening to her own words. She stepped out of bed.

★ ★ ★ ★ ★

2. THREE KEYS

★ ★ ★ ★ ★

THE SEARCH BEGAN. Mona was certain of one thing: Uncle
Florence had sought Capri in books. She opened the door
to the second bedroom, where Uncle Florence kept his
books. The floor-to-ceiling shelves sagged with books, the
long table was piled high with books: books to be mailed
to customers, books to be unwrapped and catalogued.

Which book or books?

A book Uncle Florence had recently seen, Mona
thought, or he wouldn't have left so suddenly for Capri.

Butterflies. Mona remembered the last book Florence
had shown her at the auction. She quickly dismissed the
possibility of finding Capri in a spot on a purple butterfly's wing. After all, it was a colorplate book, and colorplate books were his specialty.

Joseph Conrad. Two were still on Bargain's top shelf;

two were sitting, still wrapped, before her on the table. Uncle Florence had not read any Conrad lately, but he might have recalled some scene that described Capri. Mona sighed. She would have to read those four books, and one more. He had wanted her to read *Nig* . . . , no, *Children of the Sea.*

Resigned to a long, hard search, Mona unwrapped the auction purchases. *Youth* lay on top. She opened it and read the quotation Conrad had chosen for his title page:

> ". . . But the Dwarf answered: No; something human is dearer to me than the wealth of all the world."—GRIMM's TALES.

Mona blurted a loud sob. The dammed-up tears flooded out.

★ ★ ★ ★ ★

Mona studied each book on the table, scanned every title on the shelves. She had handled these books before, had helped catalogue them and price them. She couldn't believe they would help her find Uncle Florence's Capri.

Early the next morning she accompanied Newt to the used-car lot, and together they ransacked the Very Private Office.

"What am I looking for?" Newt asked when they were half done. Mona had not told anyone of her plan to join Uncle Florence.

"Just anything unusual," she replied, closing the closet door on the long black cloak and her memories of the Figg-Newton giant.

"How about this?" Newt held up two yellow sleeve

garters. "I wonder how they ended up in the waste basket?"

"I don't know," Mona said, but she did know. Uncle Florence no longer needed elastic bands to shorten his sleeves. He could be whoever and whatever he dreamed of being in Capri. He would never again be "almost a midget."

Except for the sleeve garters, nothing unusual was found in the shack. There was one more place to look.

"Can I have the keys to the bus, Newt?" Mona asked in a strained voice. That search had to be hers alone.

Reluctantly Newt handed her three keys on a ring.

★ ★ ★ ★ ★

Mona stumbled down the aisle of the bus, trying to ignore the cot where she had last seen her lifeless uncle. She sat down in the cold chair and focused her attention on the desk.

The top was bare. No paper was in the typewriter. One by one she emptied the drawers: business stationery, sales records, customer lists, and, lastly, a worn old book. It was the Caprification diary.

Reverently, as Uncle Florence had done so many times, Mona opened the diary and read the shaky hand-writing of Jonathan Figg:

> It was night. I was lost.
> Then I saw the tree that grows wild
> and free welcoming me with
> open arms.

She turned the page and read the flowing handwriting of Noah Figg:

The wild, free tree is only the key to the perfect dream.

She turned the page and read the flamboyant handwriting of Toby Figg:

that is standing on an island that's surrounded by the Sea.

Her hands trembling, Mona turned the page and read the new entry, written in the neat, familiar hand of Uncle Florence:

I, Florence Figg, am a bookman. I dream of a gentle world, peopled with good people and filled with simple and quiet things.

But I know little. I have had to turn to greater minds than mine.

From books I built my dream; in a book I found Capri.

I am a sick man and I shall soon go there. My dream is such a small one that perhaps the author will let me stay.

Mona read the words again and again, then tore her eyes from the page and gazed out of the window, trying to fight off the gnawing emptiness rising from the pit of her stomach. Newt was staring at her from his office; Fido was watching her from the entrance to the lot.

"Which book, Uncle Florence?" she sobbed in anger and frustration. "Which tree? Which tree is the key?"

Key. Mona grabbed the key ring and stared at the three keys. One key for the bus, one key for the Very Private Office. What was the third key for?

Mona resisted the temptation to ask Newt about the third key. This had been Uncle Florence's search; now it was her search. No one else was welcome in Capri.

Holding the key in readiness, Mona inched her way up the aisle of the bus. She peered under each seat, between each seat. Nothing. She looked in the overhead luggage racks. Nothing. She repeated her search back down the aisle. She crawled under the desk. Nothing. There was only one place left to look.

Mona took a deep breath and knelt down before the small cot. She lifted the madras spread.

Six-year-old · Dancing Wonder

Baby Flo

It was not a cot at all. A foam-rubber mattress lay on top of a trunk. A locked trunk.

And the key fit.

Flinging aside the mattress, she lifted the lid. Books! A trunkful of well-used books, none of which she had seen before.

*From books I built my dream;
in a book I found Capri.*

Mona tenderly removed the books one by one. Just handling them made her feel closer to Uncle Florence and his Capri.

500 Self-Portraits. Page after page of people in centuries of costumes; face after face looking out in a strangely similar three-quarter pose, as if she were their mirror. One of these faces could have been taken by Uncle Florence. One of these faces could be Uncle Florence as he now looked in Capri.

Claude Lorrain: Drawings. A large, thick book containing thousands of tiny reproductions of tree-strewn landscapes. One of them now existed in Capri.

Wonderful Characters. The frontispiece showed a woman with the head of a pig. Mona quickly decided that this book had found its way into the trunk by accident.

Songs of Innocence and Experience, by William Blake. Trianon edition. Mona flipped through the exquisitely colored pages; the words, hand-engraved in the plates, were difficult to read:

> Frowning frowning night,
> O'er the desart bright. . . .

"Mona. . . . Lunchtime." Mona jumped on hearing Newt's call. "Come, I'll take you to Flabby's for a hamburger."

Mona picked up a small pamphlet from the trunk and dashed up the aisle, meeting Newt at the bus door. She didn't want her father treading on sacred ground.

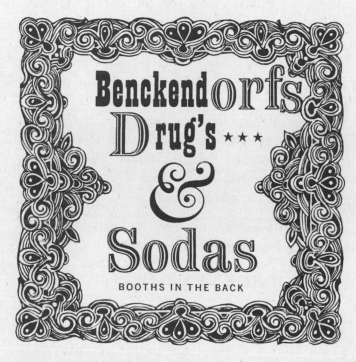

Mona ignored Flabby Benckendorf's greeting and darted into a booth.

"Hi, Flabby, same as usual, for two, and heavy on the French fries," Newt called out as he followed his daughter to the rear of the store. He sat down opposite her and read aloud from the torn pamphlet that was hiding Mona's face.

" '*Yeoman of the Guard*. Vocal Score.' Where in heaven's name did you find that? Your mother's been looking all over the place for it."

Mona couldn't believe, didn't want to believe, that Sissie knew about the secret books.

"It's Gilbert and Sullivan," Newt explained. "Your mother sang one of those songs at the funeral." He paused, hoping he hadn't said the wrong thing, but Mona was impatient to hear more.

"She sang beautifully," he continued, "slow and sad-like, but I think she must have got some of the words mixed up."

Mona wanted to hear the song.

Newt waited until Flabby finished serving and returned to the counter; then, his mouth full of hamburger and his tie in the ketchup, he leaned over the table and sang softly and out of tune:

"When a brother leaves his sister
  For another, sister weeps,
  Tears that trickle, ears that blister,
  'Tis just pickles sister keeps."

Mona groaned.

★ "*That Sister Newton,*" *the people of Pineapple said.* "*Imagine singing about pickles at a funeral. Her poor brother's funeral, at that. And Newton ("Newt") Newton's too dumb to even be embarrassed. Figgs!*"

"Hey, Newt, I didn't know you could sing. Ha, ha!" Bump Popham slapped Newt on the back with such good-natured force that a smaller man would have been dumped on Mona's lap. "Mind if I join you?"

Not waiting for an invitation, the coach eased into the booth next to Mona, who grudgingly moved closer to the wall. Newt was done with singing for a while, so the talk turned to Fido.

"Nothing wrong with his arm," Bump complained. "It's his head that worries me. In his last game before quitting the team, he struck a kid out on three pitches. Then he throws another pitch and catches the home-plate umpire smack in the head. Maybe you know what's the matter with him, huh, Mona?" The coach jabbed Mona with his elbow, knocking the pamphlet out of her hands. It landed open before her on the table.

SONG.—PHOEBE.
Were I thy bride,
Then all the world beside
    Were not too wide
      to hold my wealth of love—
Were I thy bride!

Phoebe! If Phoebe really existed, how could she be in Capri? On the other hand, if Uncle Florence had invented her. . . . Mona closed the pamphlet angrily. "Here, Newt, give this to Mom."

"Hey, Mona, you're looking pretty good," Bump Popham said. "Looks like you lost some weight."

"We'd better be getting back," Newt said, rising. This was not the time to discuss Mona's new figure.

★ ★ ★ ★ ★

Mona, back in the bus, dug deeper into the trunk. She opened each book cautiously now, stung by her discovery of Phoebe's Song.

Colorplate books: violets, hummingbirds, peach trees and plum trees, cottages and country furniture.

Another songbook: Schubert for voice and piano.

Literature: Chaucer, Dickens, Hawthorne, Dostoevski, Conrad. . . .

Mona stared in disbelief at the familiar book in her hand. Joseph Conrad. *Typhoon*. Dark green binding, decorated cloth with a slight tear at the top of the spine.

Frantically she dug through the remainder of books in the trunk and found the other first edition.

Typhoon. Lord Jim. She had thought these two books were still on old man Bargain's top shelf, yet here they were in her hands. Uncle Florence could not reach the top shelf by himself, and they had not worn the giant disguise since the day she first saw these Conrads, since the day she took down the Spanish map. . . .

"Las Hazanas Fantasticas!" Mona exclaimed aloud. She furiously searched through the books. *Las Hazañas Fantásticas* was not in the trunk. It was not in the bus.

★ ★ ★ ★ ★

Sissie was pounding the piano and the sanitation department was practicing a Highland fling when Mona hurtled into the book room.

Again she scanned every title on the shelves. Again she rummaged through the books on the table. *Las Hazañas Fantásticas* was not in the house. Stopping her ears with her fingers, Mona tried to think. She was utterly confused, and Scottish garbage men didn't help.

There was only one more place to look. Mona grabbed *Sex Histories of American College Men* off a shelf and ran back to the used-car lot.

Fido was staring at the green bus, as Mona had expected.

"Here," she said, handing him the book. "You can keep it."

Fido leafed through its pages with such lack of interest that Mona thought she had taken the wrong book in her haste.

"Fido, will you do me a huge favor?" Mona asked sweetly. "Please."

3. CREEPING, CRAWLING

THE GROTESQUE GIANT in tattered black cloak, blue jeans, and sneakers staggered down Hemlock Street. Mrs. Lumpholtz, thinking she had seen a ghost, ran shrieking into Harriet Kluttz, Hair Sets and Cuts. The giant, taller than ever, ducked into Bargain Books.

Old man Bargain was perched on his high stool under the hanging light bulb, engrossed in a book. Mona kept her eyes glued to his shining bald spot as the giant lurched toward the back shelves.

Fido remembered his instructions well. The giant inched along the stacks on the back wall as Mona matched the titles against her memory. *The Romance of Sandwich Glass* was still on the top shelf with the rest of the "retirement investment," but the two Conrads were gone. Another book was in their place.

Trembling with excitement, Mona lunged for *Las Ha-*

zañas Fantásticas, thrusting Fido off-balance. He crashed to the floor as Mona, with a desperate effort, caught the edge of the high shelf and hung, feet dangling in space. Fido picked himself up and dashed out of the shop.

Her fingers slipping, her feet groping for a foothold on a lower shelf, Mona peered over her shoulder at the grumpy shopkeeper. The bald spot was gone. Old man Bargain had raised his head and was waving a notebook at her threateningly. It was her Figg-Newton composition. Uttering a cry of surprise, Mona dropped to the floor and, clutching the long cloak around her waist, ran out of the store, down the street, around the corner, and through the used-car lot into Newt's office.

"Hi, princess, look what I discovered." Smiling triumphantly, Newt held up the open pamphlet of *Yeoman of the Guard*. "It wasn't 'pickles sister keeps' at all. Look, it says:

"Tears that trickle, tears that blister—
'Tis but mickle sister reaps!"

Mona slid to the floor, pulled her knees up to her chest, and buried her face in her arms. Pickle, mickle, Conrad, Supuesto, Phoebe, Fido. She raised her head and shouted, "That rotten Fido. That dog of a rotten Fido. That rotten dumb-headed dog of a Fido!"

"I wonder what 'mickle' means," Newt replied.

★ ★ ★ ★ ★

Sissie and Newt were singing a duet from the pamphlet. Stretched out and sunk in the broken springs of the couch, Mona was trying to read "Heart of Darkness" from one of her auction purchases. Mona loved to handle books, to examine and catalogue them, but reading them was difficult, particularly with the silly noises her parents were making:

> "Like a ghost his vigil keeping—
> Or a spectre all-appalling—
> I beheld a figure creeping.
> I should rather call it crawling."

Fido stood in the doorway unnoticed. He blew his nose softly.

Mona read and reread each phrase with care, weighed every word for a clue.

> "It seems to me I am trying to tell you a dream—making a vain attempt, because no relation of a dream can convey the dream sensation, that commingling of absurdity, surprise, and bewilderment in a tremor of struggling revolt . . . that notion of being captured by the incredible which is of the very essence of dreams. . . ."

" 'He was creeping,' " Sissie sang.

" 'He was crawling,' " Newt sang.

" 'He was creeping, creeping,' " sang Sissie.

" 'Crawling!' " sang Newt, lunging toward Mona with clawlike hands.

Mona screamed.

"Gee, princess, I didn't mean to scare you," Newt said sheepishly, but Mona was more frightened by a sentence she had just read:

> "We live, as we dream—alone."

Mona slammed the book shut. She refused to believe it had anything to do with Capri.

Fido joined in the apologizing. "Mona, I'm really sorry about this afternoon at Bargain's."

The Newtons spun around, surprised to see a visitor.

"Fido, you're a . . . ," Mona paused. "Fido, you owe me a lot of favors."

Fido nodded in agreement.

" 'Sing me your song, O!' " Newt sang in a booming bass-baritone. Sissie had found another duet and was thumping out the melody on the piano, waiting for her own solo.

Heads together, Mona and Fido entered into a new conspiracy. Mona talked; Fido nodded. He promised to read the Conrad books and report on each one to her. Mona explained, with some pride, that the books were rare and expensive first editions. Fido promised to handle them with care and not take them out of the house.

> "It is sung to the moon
> By a love-lorn loon,
> Who fled from the mocking throng, O!"

Fido looked up to watch Sissie singing lustily and dancing an energetic soft-shoe.

"Go wash your hands and wipe your nose, Fido," Mona commanded.

Fido obeyed his new mistress. When he returned, she presented him with *Lord Jim.*

Fido read, and Mona thought. She had to find a way of getting *Las Hazañas Fantásticas* off that top shelf. Suddenly Newt sang his chorus with such ear-shattering enthusiasm that they both jumped.

> "Heighdy! heighdy!
> Misery me, lackadaydee!"

"That's supposed to be a sad song," Mona suggested. "Sad and quiet."

"I like it that way, Uncle Newt," Fido said. Mona glared at her slave, who cast his eyes down on *Lord Jim*.

"I like it that way, too," Sissie said. "I think you're doing just fine, Newt."

"You mean it?" Newt asked. "But maybe we should find a different song for Mona."

All was quiet while Sissie riffled through the score. Then the singing began again.

> "The prisoner comes to meet his doom;
> The block, the headsman, and the tomb.
> The funeral bell begins to toll—
> May Heaven have mercy on his soul."

"Oh no," Mona moaned.

"Well, you asked for a sad song," Sissie said.

"It's sad, all right," Fido said, tears streaming down his cheeks. He decided he would have to do his reading somewhere else.

★ ★ ★ ★ ★

Days passed. Days devoted to poring over secret books and skulking around Bargain Books. Mona was desperate. She expected to fail English if she wasn't first arrested for tampering with the mails or embarrassed to death during the Founders' Day parade when her parents would sing and dance down Hemlock Street before the smirking people of Pineapple.

It was more than Mona could bear. She missed Uncle Florence more deeply every day. She had to find Capri, and soon.

If only Fido could read faster, she thought. He had finished one book, *Lord Jim*, and his report consisted of one word: Jump.

Mona stared at one of the secret books opened to a colorplate of a ruby-throated hummingbird. If only she could get the copy of Pirata Supuesto's *Las Hazanas* from old man Bargain's top shelf.

That was it! A copy! She didn't need a first edition; a second printing, a later edition, a facsimile, any copy would do.

4. A GARISH FACSIMILE

FIDO WAS sprawled out at a table reading a later edition of *Typhoon* when Mona burst into the library and descended on the card-catalogue cabinet. She yanked out the drawers, one by one, and anxiously thumbed through the listings.

STA–SUZ . . . . No "Supuesto."

LAB–LED . . . . No "Las Hazanas."

HAB–HEX . . . . No "Hazanas."

FAL–FRO . . . . No "Fantasticas."

One more try and then she would have to ask the librarian's help and involve still another person in her dream search.

MAB–MAR. Maps. Maps, Spanish.

There was no reference to her book, but she found one promising title.

526.8
G

MAPS. Spanish.

Five centuries of Spanish maps.
Compiler and editor: J. Garcia y Lopez.
London. Paradise Press, 1912.

Facsimiles of Spanish maps from books
of the fourteenth through nineteenth
centuries. i–viii. 640 p. 532 illus.

○

Mona jotted down the code number and with a trembling hand presented it to Miss Quigley. "Why hello,
Mona. I haven't seen you in ages. You don't look well,
dear," the librarian said.

"I've been sick," Mona replied, pale with impatience.

"I'm sorry to hear that." Miss Quigley read the request.
"No one has asked for this book in a long time. I'll have
someone look for it in the stacks. You'd better sit down;
it may take a while."

Mona didn't want to sit down. Knuckles white from
clutching the edge of the desk, she stood, waiting, waiting,
for the map book to appear. Miss Quigley finished stamp-
ing some books and returned to chat.

"I didn't know you were interested in maps."

Mona turned her back on the librarian with a pretense of coughing, trying to think of a convincing fib.
She saw Fido, his nose running, his lips moving as he read,
and spun around.

"Miss Quigley, would you, by any chance, have a book
by Joseph Conrad called *Children of the Sea*?"

"*Children of the Sea?* No, I don't think so." The

assistant librarian emerged from the stacks and handed the book of Spanish maps to Miss Quigley, who was still musing on Conrad titles. "I think you must mean *Mirror of the Sea.*"

"No, that's a different book," Mona replied curtly, her eyes riveted on the map book in the librarian's hand. "I want *Children of the Sea,* or *Nigger. . . .*"

Mona spit out the hateful word and with a horror of sudden awareness, recognized that Miss Quigley—Miss Quigley, who had read stories aloud to her before she could read, Miss Quigley, who had recommended books to her, had searched for books for her, had discussed books with her—that Miss Quigley was black.

Rebecca Quigley's face froze in pained shock. Mona grabbed the book of Spanish maps from her hand and fled from the library sobbing.

★ ★ ★ ★ ★

The Chamber of Commerce was tapping to "There's No Business Like Show Business."

"Hi, Mona, look at me," shuffling Flabby Benckendorf shouted.

Mona stumbled up the stairs, still sobbing, and flung herself onto her bed. She sobbed out of loneliness and fear and confusion; and for once she sobbed for someone other than herself. Unthinkingly she had hurt Miss Quigley. She could never face the librarian again. "I wish I were dead," she moaned aloud. "I wish I were with you, Uncle Florence. I wish I were in Capri."

Capri.

Mona sat up and fumbled for the book of facsimile maps. Drying her eyes with her sleeve, she searched the table of contents.

The Chamber of Commerce had given way to the Horticultural Society, tiptoeing through the tulips. The Horticultural Society had given way to thirty kindergarten children tap-dancing and screeching "On the Good Ship Lollipop."

Mona lay across her bed, her chin cupped in her hand, her eyes smarting, a finger tracing and retracing every outline on the garishly colored facsimile map. She pored over each line, each speck, wishing, hoping. At last her finger came to rest on a tiny, irregularly shaped island. On it was a tree. A palm, a pink palm.

Mona read the name: Capri.

"Mona, wait!" Fido shouted, bursting into her room, waving the book Miss Quigley had lent him: *The Nigger of the Narcissus.* "Mona," Fido cried, "the book says: Wait!"

"Mona, wake up, wake up." Fido shook his sleeping cousin.

Sissie, standing in the doorway, screamed.

⭐ ⭐ ⭐ ⭐ ⭐

1. THE PINK PALM

⭐ ⭐ ⭐ ⭐ ⭐

MONA FLOATED through a swirling nothingness, through doorless doors and windowless windows, into the eye of a windless storm. Then all was still.

Colors pulsated from orange to pink as she gazed up into the fronds of a palm tree.

" 'The tree that is wild and free,' " she murmured. "Capri. I am in Capri."

The palm tree replied with a blaze of pink.

Weary from her long, roadless journey, Mona leaned against the palm, waiting for the familiar figure of her Uncle Florence, or the form he had now taken as his own, to appear on the horizon.

There was no horizon. The gray sky, if there was a sky, was bound to the gray land by an invisible seam. All was silent.

"An island that's surrounded by the sea," Mona remembered, and then she heard the sea washing unseen rocks on an unseen shore. Undulating. Surging. Pounding. Faster, faster the waves crashed and thundered; the ground shuddered, beaten by an angry foam.

Orange blotches again mottled the palm's thrashing fronds, spreading its color as if to devour the pink. Lashed by the winds, Mona wrapped her arms around the swaying trunk. Some invisible power was trying to tear her from the tree. Some force was trying to blow her back into endless space. Mona refused to go.

"Pink palm, pink palm," she cried over and over as she hung on to the one tangible reality in her unformed dream. At last the storm subsided; the waters calmed. The orange blight faded, and once again the palm stood tall and pink.

★ ★ ★ ★ ★

Exhausted and confused, Mona sank to her knees and rested her head against her palm tree. Where was Uncle Florence? Who was trying to frighten her? Was she really in Capri or was she lost in her own nightmare? Lost.

"It was night. I was lost." As Mona remembered the words of the diary, the gray darkened to starless night. Black, impenetrable night that only magnified her fears. She tried to think of something to free her mind from the terrors that lurk in the night. She remembered a small book in the secret hoard; she remembered the blue in the illustration bordering a poem; she remembered trying to decipher the cramped lettering. And then she remembered these words:

Frowning frowning night,
O'er the desert bright,
Let thy moon arise
While I close my eyes.

Mona opened her eyes to the dark blue of the sky. A full moon nested in the "welcoming arms" of the pink palm. From afar she heard the lapping sea, and from farther still, the faint tap-tap-tapping of dancing feet.

"Uncle Florence," Mona shouted, but no figure crossed the moonlit sands. The tapping faded away.

Mona rose and started across the desert in search of her phantom uncle.

★ ★ ★ ★ ★

The moon glowed brightly, hotter and hotter, until it blazed into the ball of a scorching sun.

Mona squinted back at the far-off palm, now suffused with orange light, then slogged on through the heat and glare. Her feet sank deeper into the sand with each step; a searing wind penetrated her every pore. Something more than the blistering heat and sucking sand was trying to hold her back.

Defiant, her mouth parched, her tongue swollen, Mona shouted her mother's song:

" 'Twas on the Isle of Capri
That I met her,
'Neath the shade
Of an old apple tree. . . ."

Mona shouted—and remembered. There had been an apple tree in her yard at home, an old, twisted apple tree no longer bearing fruit. She knew it well, having stared at its leaves so often from her bedroom window.

Now she stared at the apple tree again as it rose in all its knotted glory before her.

The grass was long and cool in the shade of the old apple tree. Mona wished for a tall glass of lemonade, and it appeared in her hand. She took a tasteless sip, then recalled the tart, thirst-quenching flavor and drank deeply.

Leaning back refreshed, reveling in her new-found power of wishes-come-true, Mona laughed with delight. She knew what her next wish would be.

★ ★ ★ ★ ★

Mona gazed into the desolation bordering her apple-tree world, wishing. Wishing. Wishing.

Slowly he appeared, a four-foot six-inch shadow shaped by remembered details: the round face, the sad smile, the graying hair, the gnarled hands. The yellow sleeve garters.

Mona hid her face in her hands and dismissed the vision. Uncle Florence had not taken his sleeve garters with him; he had long arms now, he was taller, different. She had to find him as he was now, as he looked now, in his own dream, in his own Capri.

Mona set one foot on the scorching sand and withdrew it. Her journey might be a long one; she needed one more wish.

Closing her eyes, she wished for a horse, a big, black stallion to carry her over the boundless desert. Then she opened her eyes. Before her limped a formless black mass with flowing mane, a misshapen body on misplaced legs.

Mona quickly erased the hideous animal from sight and tried again to picture a horse. Straining her memory, she tried to visualize where the eyes were in relation to the nostrils, how the head joined the neck, where the legs met the body. It was hopeless. Mona had looked at many horses, but she had never truly seen one.

She would have to travel on foot, tomorrow. Another frowning night was blinding the desert, still burning under a darkened sun. Again Mona closed her eyes, recited the Blake poem, and opened them to a full moon— and words, suspended in space.

Mona
GO BACK!
&
GOME HOME
WE MISS YO

"I won't, I won't go back," she shouted.

An ominous cloud crept over Mona's moon, shrouding her in blackness. The sign vibrated like a banged sheet of tin and shattered. Its drumming echoes bounced off the wall of night.

"Uncle Florence, where are you?"

The answer was a deafening thunderclap that rocked the ground. A bolt of lightning tore the sky and set fires dancing in a circle around her refuge.

Sobbing in defeat, Mona stumbled back toward the distant palm, her path lighted by the apple tree burning behind her.

★ ★ ★ ★ ★

2. THE GREEN DUNGEON

★ ★ ★ ★ ★

THE PINK-ORANGE PALM had multiplied into a green jungle. Orchids burst from mossy trunks; a cockatoo called. Mona stood in awe before the nameless fruits and perfumed flowers. She had never seen such wild beauty, not at home, not in books . . . and then she remembered the words Uncle Florence had written in the diary:

> . . . a gentle world, peopled with good people and filled with simple and quiet things.

This exotic paradise had not been created by Uncle Florence. Terrified, Mona spun around. Her way was barred by a thicket of tortured mangroves. The green dungeon was guarded by strangler vines and domed by a web of locked branches.

Mona was trapped in someone else's dream!

Triangles of apple-tree fire flickered through giant ferns; a parrot mocked her sobs. Suddenly something grasped at Mona's ankle, and she fell among the tangled vines. Among the writhing roots. Among the snakes.

Choking with terror, she felt the snakes creeping, crawling over her legs.

> They were creeping,
>   They were crawling,
> They were creeping, creeping—
>   Crawling!

Mona looked down at the vines twisted around her ankle. Vines, not snakes. The snakes had been the reflection of her own fears, the distorted memory of her parents' duet.

Trembling uncontrollably, Mona laughed and cried in a confusion of emotions. Her blood drummed in her ears in time with the distant tapping. At last she lay back, limp and silent.

How strange that her fears were stronger than her dreams, she thought, the snakes more real than the unrealized horse. Mona looked about her. Perhaps the jungle, too, was painted out of fear. Closing her eyes, Mona willed the vines and the trees and the ferns to disappear.

The jungle remained, and she remained its prisoner, shackled by vines, watched by a pair of gleaming eyes.

Someone or something was near. Slowly Mona raised her head. A strangled cry escaped from her lips as she stared into the unblinking eyes of a leopard crouched on an overhanging limb.

Straining at her vine-bound ankle, Mona tried to will the animal away as another incarnation of her own fear. The leopard hunched forward, ready to spring.

The phantom of a leopard was about to savage the phantom of a young girl.

"But I'm not alive," Mona shouted, convincing herself of her own invulnerability. "I am dead and can't be harmed. I am in Capri!"

The leopard eyes narrowed in anger. From somewhere, from everywhere, a thundering voice replied:

> "Where all life dies, death lives,
>   and Nature breeds,
> Perverse, all monstrous, all prodigious things.
> Abominable, inutterable, and worse
> Than fables yet have feigned,
>   or fear conceived,
> Gorgons and Hydras, and Chimeras dire."

A deathly chill crept over Mona's flesh as, unable to move, unable to scream, she watched the leopard change form.

Its rosettes spun like pinwheels; its bulk exceeded its frame. And still it grew. The formless shadow floated toward her, its armless arms outstretched in a ghostly transfiguration of night. Then, with a flash of teeth and a glint of steel, the monstrous being gathered its substance into the shape of a magnificent wild-eyed man.

"Uncle Florence?" Mona muttered hoarsely in the desperate hope that this was her uncle's new form. "Uncle Florence, it's me, Mona," she babbled. "Uncle Florence?"

"No," the pirate roared, his teeth bared in anger and his black hair flying in a sudden howl of wind. Leopard eyes ablaze, he unsheathed his sword and flourished its razor-sharp blade.

Mona tore wildly at the tangled growth.

Tap-tap-tap echoed from the distance.

Tap-tap-tappity-tap-tap. The noise rose to a clattering crescendo.

With an agonized yell the pirate clapped his hands to his ears. His sword fell, slashing through the vines around Mona's leg.

Free, afraid to look back, Mona fled down the path that opened before her feet, trampling flowers and ferns as she ran toward the tapping, her arms held out trying to clutch the sound of the dancing feet.

★ ★ ★ ★ ★

Tap-tap-tappity-tap. A blurred face appeared in the whiteness. Someone was holding Mona's hand.

"Uncle Florence," Mona cried, straining to sit up. Still entangled in vines, she fell back into the soft sand. "Uncle Florence," she whispered as the face faded into the fronds of the pink palm.

★ ★ ★ ★ ★

Alone, bound only by the unknown, Mona sat up and stared into the curtained wilderness. She shuddered as she remembered the jungle of yesterday. Or was it a century ago? Shaking her head free of doubt and nightmare terrors, she struggled to think only of Uncle Florence. Not of his physical presence (she could not even guess at that), but of his hopes, his loves, his dream of "simple and quiet things."

A butterfly lighted on her shoulder and flitted away. Mona watched its colors change subtly from lavender to purple to violet.

★ ★ ★ ★ ★

The butterfly fluttered through the peach trees and plum trees and disappeared. Mona crossed a Claude Lorrain landscape and walked through a small village. The streets were deserted; its shops empty.

She turned the corner at Hemlock and Ash as the large mahogany doors of the opera house were closing. Mona was the last in a long line of shadowy shapes that climbed the carpeted stairway into a huge, triple-tiered auditorium. Crystal chandeliers twinkled from the gilt ceiling, then dimmed as Mona felt her way to a plush seat in the middle of the back row. She wished she had remembered to buy a box of popcorn on the way in.

The red velvet curtain parted to reveal a grand piano on the center of a bare stage. A man and a woman in formal dress emerged from the wings and bowed to the welcoming applause.

A box flew out of Mona's hand, raining popcorn on the neighboring shadows. "Uncle Florence!" Mona shouted, but invisible bonds held her in her seat. Her cry went unnoticed; the show was about to begin and nothing could stop it.

The man sat down at the piano, flexed his long fingers, and placed his gracefully arched hands on the keys. He played brilliantly. Mona recognized the left-hand accompaniment to Schubert's "Who Is Sylvia?"

Uncle Florence looked remarkably unchanged, Mona thought. He was perhaps slightly younger, and his feet reached the pedals of the piano, but she was certain that she was not dreaming him this time. She never would have invited Phoebe to Capri.

Phoebe. Mona studied the singer with a critical eye. She wasn't beautiful, but she was surely handsome, even noble, and glowing with warmth. Mona could not tell whether Phoebe was four-feet four-inches tall, but she was shorter than Uncle Florence. Standing side by side they bowed to thunderous applause. Mona's jealousy turned to smugness as she realized that Phoebe's presence in Capri proved that Uncle Florence had invented her. He had invented Phoebe to keep him company until Mona arrived in his dream.

Now Florence sang while Phoebe accompanied his mighty bass-baritone on the piano. The Schubert cycle had never before been sung with such artistry, and for the first time Mona understood the German words.

> "And our grieving,
> Tears relieving,
> Purify from earthly stain,
> Borne to heaven, then forgiven,
> Tears eternal life obtain,
> Tears eternal life obtain."

Basking in her uncle's magnificent performance, Mona imagined his delight on discovering her here in Capri. Her tears were a thing of the past, and she would now re-place her stand-in, Phoebe, and live with Florence for the rest of their eternal lives.

The recital ended to a standing ovation. The audi-ence flowed into the aisles, cheering, applauding. Mona struggled in vain to get through.

At last the curtains closed on the flower-strewn stage

as the singers took their fiftieth bow. The lights went up; the audience turned to leave, and Mona now saw their familiar faces in three-quarter view.

Pushing her way past the five hundred self-portraits, past the woman with the head of a pig, climbing over row after row of seats, clambering up the steps, Mona called to her uncle. She ducked under the curtain; the stage was bare. She ran through the wings, flung open the stage door, and blinked into the sun.

Uncle Florence and Phoebe were strolling hand-in-hand through a field of violets. A ruby-throated humming-bird flitted around their heads.

"Uncle Florence," Mona shouted.

Her way was blocked by a monstrous shadow brandishing a sword.

★ ★ ★ ★ ★

The menacing pirate of Mona's nightmare moved toward her, the shadow of his shadow creeping over her feet. Suddenly he stopped, grimaced in pain, and held his hands over his ears.

Tap-tap-tappity-tap-tap. Mona heard it, too, and took advantage of her tormentor's torment to slip out of his presence. Quickly she ducked into a dimly lit shop, slamming the door so violently that a book fell from the top shelf.

Ebenezer Bargain swore softly and bent down to pick up the fallen book. The light from the shop's single bulb reflected off his silver hair.

Her hands behind her clutching the doorknob, Mona watched the old bookseller resume his perch on the high stool. He no longer had his bald spot; otherwise he, too, appeared unchanged. And he, too, must have studied the map in *Las Hazañas Fantásticas* before he died.

Resentful of old man Bargain, fearful of the savage pirate in the street, Mona tried to think of Uncle Florence, only of Uncle Florence. Slowly the knob turned in her hand. Once again she stood behind the opera house and saw Phoebe and Uncle Florence in the field of flowers.

"Uncle Florence!" Mona shouted.

A hand gripped her shoulder.

"No!" The pirate's voice was deep and stern. "No, let them be."

★ ★ ★ ★ ★

3. SOMEONE ELSE'S DREAM

★ ★ ★ ★ ★

MONA SAT on the edge of a large carved chair, her eyes trying to escape the pirate's intent stare. Fear had given way to confusion; unasked questions were stuck in her throat.

At last the pirate spoke. "Seems rather damp in here," he said with surprising mildness.

Now Mona felt the dampness and nodded in agreement. The pirate fanned the flames in the great marble fireplace and began pacing the palatial room. Mona wished she were sitting on something more comfortable.

"Get that monstrosity out of my castle," the pirate shouted as she snuggled into the broken springs of her old sofa. Mona quickly sat upright again in the carved chair. "I'm sorry," she whispered hoarsely.

"I haven't decided on all the furnishings for this

room," he said, softening his tone again, "but that sofa was ridiculous, absolutely ridiculous."

Trembling, Mona nodded again and racked her brains for something to say, something casual and pleasant. She knew instinctively that she would have to please her eccentric captor if she were going to reach Uncle Florence. Clearing her throat, she made an awkward attempt at polite conversation. "How many rooms do you have here?"

"It varies," the pirate replied. "Anywhere from fifteen to one hundred and eighty-five, depending on my mood."

"I'd guess there are about fifteen rooms now," Mona said, familiar with his wild swings of temperament.

"You're probably right. I do feel in a fifteen-room mood. Fifteen rooms, that is, not counting the sapphire ballroom I built for Phoebe and Florence. They love to dance, you know." Anticipating Mona's next question, he turned away.

"We'll discuss that later."

Mona would have to wait, but she wanted to keep her host in his fifteen-room mood. He was still wearing a sword, and his hand rested on the jeweled hilt. "How many bedrooms do you have?" she asked. It was the wrong question.

"None!" The pirate's face darkened as he pointed threateningly at Mona. "No bedrooms; no sleep; no dreams. Not while I have a stubborn, heartless intruder on my island.

"I have had to watch your every clumsy step. I have had to listen to your whining cries and that ear-shattering tapping that follows you everywhere. I have had to blot out your philistine wishes and tasteless encroachments, your appleless apple tree and your crudely drawn sign."

"But I didn't make that sign." Mona's protest went unheard as the pirate ranted on.

"I have had to resort to threats and terrors, heat and hurricanes and the tongue of John Milton, and still you remain, uninvited, unwanted, a blemish on this, my most magnificent dream of dreams."

"This is NOT your dream," Mona shouted, fearless with rage.

The pirate laughed a loud, mocking laugh.

"I belong here!" Mona screamed, lashing back at the pirate as she had wanted to lash back at the people of Pineapple. "I belong here, here in Capri with Uncle Florence and my pink palm."

"Pink!" His leopard eyes glared. The pirate seized Mona by the arm and dragged her across the marble floor to the high arched window. "Look! Look at your pink palm."

Alone on a stretch of sand in the distance the tall palm glowed a muted orange.

"The color is coral, coral, a delicate shade of coral. Not PINK!" He clenched his teeth on the word pink as if to gnash it apart, then, his poise regained, continued. "That CORAL palm was drawn by my own hand, painted with my own brush, on my own island, on my own map, in my own book: *The Imaginary Adventures of a Would-Be Pirate.*"

"But the book was in Spanish," Mona challenged feebly.

"I am speaking Spanish," replied the would-be pirate.

★ ★ ★ ★ ★

The Spanish map-maker and would-be pirate, Capitán Miguel de Caprichos, sat at the head of the banquet table waited on by faceless servants. At the foot of the long board Mona poked at her food, tortured by humiliation and uncertainty.

"Eat," he commanded. "You must be strong for your trip back."

"Back where?" Mona asked dejectedly.

"What did you say?"

"I said, back where? Why did you dream up such a huge table for only two people? If I were dreaming up a dining room, I would put in. . . ."

"You would put in what?" Her host was open to suggestion.

Mona didn't know. She had never paid much attention to furniture, or houses, or horses. "I'd just have a smaller table," she replied humbly.

"Is that better?" he asked.

The table shrank in size; silver platters of food tumbled to the floor and vanished.

Mona smiled and wished herself a hamburger from Flabby's. And a candle for the middle of the table.

"Very good. You don't look half as scraggly by candlelight."

Mona had forgotten what she looked like. She had never been pleased with her appearance, but now that she could be whoever she wanted to be, she felt most comfortable inside her ordinary, everyday body, with all its faults. At least it was hers. Nothing else in this ghostly land was hers, not even the pink palm. Not even Uncle Florence.

"Cheer up," the pirate ordered. "Gloom is not allowed

on Caprichos. You do understand that you will have to return to your home. You don't belong here."

"But Uncle Florence. . . ."

"Florence and Phoebe will remain. They are knowledgeable and talented citizens, and companionable neighbors. I have learned a great deal from them." He dismissed the subject with a monologue on candles and candlesticks.

"There is a gold candelabrum, studded with emeralds and rubies, on a treasure ship I almost captured. I was defeated by Admiral One-Eye, an admirable adversary, but his ship will pass this way again. Then victory may be mine."

"That's the silliest thing I've ever heard," Mona said. "Losing a battle in your own dream."

"Defeat makes the final victory all the sweeter," the would-be pirate explained. "In real life sweet moments are short and dulled by time. But here the mind can invent and reinvent. Here I can relive each battle until I have perfected every detail of my glorious triumphs."

"That's childish," Mona said, remembering with shame her childish parents. "Uncle Florence isn't childish."

"Your charming uncle and my dearest friend, Florence Figg," the pirate replied, "has married Phoebe twenty-six times since arriving in Caprichos."

★ ★ ★ ★ ★

Capitán Miguel de Caprichos rose from the table. "It is time for you to go."

"No, please," Mona begged. "Please let me see Uncle Florence."

The would-be pirate was firm.

"Then let me stay here," Mona begged.

"And what can you contribute here? A broken-down sofa, a hamburger, a candle?"

"Books. I know books. I can build you a library."

"Come," the captain said. Mona followed him into his library. Mahogany cases with glass-enclosed shelves lined the paneled room, filled with rare and exquisite volumes.

"Make me a book," he commanded.

Mona strained her memory for a book, a book he had never seen, a book that would delight him. Ships, exotic scenes.

The remembered first edition—dark green binding—decorated cloth—slight tear in . . . (no, Mona quickly repaired the torn backstrap) . . . slowly materialized in her hands. She presented it to her captor.

The pirate turned to the frontispiece illustration of a ship in a raging storm and smiled. He read aloud from the title page. "Typhoon, by Joseph Conrad."

Mona breathed a sigh of relief; he could read English after all, or some language common to dreams. But as the would-be pirate turned the pages, a scowl distorted his handsome face. He slammed the book shut and thrust it back into her hands.

"This is not a book," he growled. "This is a package. A package of nothing."

Hands shaking, Mona examined her book. Except for the memorized title, not a word appeared on any page. She stared down at her unread blank pages. "I want to see Uncle Florence. Please," she begged, and burst into tears.

Torn between anger and pity, the pirate remained

silent. He placed a hand on her trembling shoulder. "All right, you poor, dreamless, unchildlike child," he said at last. "Dry those sightless eyes. I will let you see Florence once more. Just once more. But . . . he must not know who you are.

"He must not know who you are."

★ ★ ★ ★ ★

4. THE LAST DANCE

★ ★ ★ ★ ★

COLORED LANTERNS danced on a string around the ter-
raced balcony; brilliant orchids studded the jungle canopy
below. Mona wished up a fruit bowl full of figs and pineapples for the table decoration. This was to be her last
night in Capitán Miguel de Caprichos' dream, and although she had promised not to reveal her identity when
Uncle Florence arrived, she was determined to give him
clues.

"Now, what shall we call you?" the pirate mused.

Mona thought of a Conrad title. "Narcissus. It's my
favorite flower," she lied. "Narcissus Q. Holtzlump."

"Ridiculous. You shall be Señorita Narcissus Maria-
Teresa Murillo y Olivares de Santiago. And twenty-three
years old."

"I don't know how to be twenty-three years old,"

Mona complained. "And I'll never remember such a long name."

"You don't have to remember it, unless you plan to spend the entire evening talking to yourself. Now make yourself taller."

"Why do I have to be taller? Phoebe's shorter than I am, and. . . ."

"Taller, seven inches taller, you obstinate child," the pirate insisted. "Why should I invent a short companion when I'm over six feet tall?"

Mona grew, looking up, looking into the rugged face of the dream-maker. "Did you look the same in real life?" she asked in admiration.

"I look exactly as I did at the age of thirty," he replied.

"How old were you when you died?"

"Old. I lived a long life, learned and loved many things. And so should you."

"You mean I can come back?" The pirate didn't answer. "I'll learn everything there is to learn; I'll look at everything there is to see. I'm a good memorizer, just like my Uncle Romulus, the Walking Book of Knowledge."

The pirate did not seem overjoyed at the prospect of seeing Mona again. "Pile your stringy hair on top of your head and wear a long white dress," he ordered.

Mona felt like the Statue of Liberty in one of Sissie's tableaus.

The pirate frowned. "Can't you put some flounces on the sleeves and hem? You are the dumpiest guest I ever had. Never mind, your compassionate uncle invites even stranger-looking guests, poor souls who found no happiness in life."

Mona thought of the pig-faced woman as her host

studied her with a critical eye. "Try, at least, to look a bit older."

"Maybe if I put a few worry lines in my face. . . ."

"You have too many worry lines now. Try to look serene, confident. Try to look like a real person."

"I am a real person," Mona insisted.

"You are a selfish, stubborn, self-centered child," the would-be pirate replied.

★ ★ ★ ★ ★

A gong reverberated through the marble corridors. The guests had arrived, singing.

> "—Hurrah for our Pirate King!
> And it is, it is a glorious thing
> To be a Pirate King!
> It is!
> —Hurrah for our Pirate King."

The pirate king strode with open arms to greet his guests. His clothes faded and he emerged from the shadowy envelope dressed in a gleaming black suit with white ruff, ruffled cuffs, and silver-buckled knee breeches.

"Dear Phoebe. Florence, my friend. Thank you for coming. May I introduce Señorita Narcissus Maria-Teresa Murillo y Olivares de Santiago."

The tall señorita presented a hand to her bowing uncle. She had planned to whisper her identity in his ear, but Florence was still only four-feet six-inches tall. And her captor was watching her with an alert eye. "You must be Florence Figg. I've heard so much about you. Delighted, I'm sure."

Florence kissed her hand politely and introduced his wife. Mona nodded in haughty recognition, then strode past Phoebe, head held high.

"Please join us on the terrace for some refreshments," Mona said with a broad gesture as she swept up the steps. The full-flounced skirt and added seven inches proved too much for Mona's fine balance. She stumbled into Phoebe's open arms.

"I'm so sorry, señorita," Mrs. Figg said sweetly. "We must have adjusted the rise of the step too quickly. It is indeed a pleasure to have such a beautiful guest visit our island."

Mona thanked Phoebe with a warm smile and studied her carefully as the pirate uncorked a bottle of champagne. Phoebe looked like Uncle Florence, acted like Uncle Florence, but was softer, tenderer. The motherly Phoebe was the female counterpart of her uncle, the part he had never allowed himself to be. Phoebe could stay, Mona decided; Phoebe and Florence would be her parents forever. And the pirate could be. . . . But she had little time left if she was to remain in Caprichos. Florence was still ignorant of her true identity.

Florence raised his glass in a toast. Mona stared hard at the glass in his hand and changed the liquid to celery tonic, her uncle's favorite soda. Mona watched for his reaction over the rim of her glass as she took her first sip of champagne.

"Ilck!" Mona uttered involuntarily, surprised by the sour taste. The pirate scowled, then forced a laugh. "Perhaps I should have served sangria to my Spanish guest."

"Or do what I do, señorita," Florence suggested. "I pretend the liquid is celery tonic. I prefer it to champagne, I'm ashamed to say. Would you like me to change yours?"

"No, thank you, I'm just fine," Mona mumbled. Her plan was faltering. Her host was angry with her.

The discussion turned to paintings for the main hall of the palace. Phoebe suggested a Gauguin. She had seen reproductions of his work in one of Florence's books and found the people beautiful, and the exotic setting would mirror the palace landscape.

Uncle Florence suggested Veláquez' "Las Meninas," one of the most glorious paintings ever created by man. "And Spanish," he added with a shy smile.

Mona gathered all of her courage. She knew the name of one painting, and now was the time to say it. "The greatest painting of all time is one with which I am quite familiar," she announced. "It is by Leonardo da Vinci, and it is called 'The Mona Lisa.' "

Mona Lisa Newton awaited her uncle's cry of recognition. Instead he and Phoebe regarded their host anxiously.

The would-be pirate calmly explained. "The señorita doesn't know. You see," he said to Mona gravely, "I had come on that very painting on a royal treasure ship. In honor of the victory I made a gift of 'The Mona Lisa' to my dear friends the Figgs."

"Mona Lisa was the name of Florence's favorite niece," Phoebe said. "And it is also the name of our two-year-old daughter." The couple smiled at each other with parental pride.

"Our little one looks just like my bride," Florence added, beaming. "I hope you'll have a chance to visit our cottage and meet her, señorita."

"No," Mona replied in a whisper. Strains of a waltz

drifted through the open French doors. "No, I'm afraid I shall be leaving soon."

The pirate ushered the Figgs into the sapphire ballroom. Mona hobbled after them and stood at the door, watching Uncle Florence and Phoebe waltzing in perfectly paired little steps, gazing lovingly into each other's eyes. Mona wanted to remember her Uncle Florence as he looked now: carefree and contented, no longer the shy, wounded creature out of place in a world too large. Uncle Florence was deservedly happy.

Blinded by tears, Mona turned to leave.

"May I have this last dance?" Capitán Miguel de Caprichos, his leopard eyes flashing, placed a strong arm around Mona's waist. He held her hand. His hand was warm, so warm. Mona spun around the floor in El Pirata Supuesto's embrace, whirling and twirling, faster, faster through a swirling nothingness.

Tap-tap-tappity-tap-tap.

★ ★ ★ ★ ★

1. WELCOME HOME

★ ★ ★ ★ ★

TAP-TAP-TAPPITY-TAP-TAP. The noise was deafening.

His hand was warm, so very warm.

Mona opened her eyes to a face in the whiteness. "Daddy," she mumbled, and tried to sit up through the tangle of tubes. Newt let go of her hand and eased her back into the pillow.

"Just lie back, princess. You're in the hospital. Sissie, come here quick," Newt shouted to his dancing and crying wife. "Mona's awake."

"My baby!" Sissie shrieked, tears streaming down her cheeks. She kissed her daughter's eyes and nose and ears and mouth, then ran out of the room to get the doctor.

Newt stroked Mona's damp hair back from her forehead. "You've been sick, princess, very sick. Everybody's been so worried. Your mother's been dancing her feet off hoping you'd hear the tapping, wherever you were, and come back to us."

"Welcome back, young lady," Dr. Davenport said, checking her vital signs and unplugging her from the machines. "I don't think you'll be needing these anymore, but I want you to lie still and rest. You set a medical record, you did. We were ready to give up on you days ago, but your father wouldn't let us. Over his dead body, he said. You must be the stubbornest critter on the face of this earth."

Sissie kissed Mona again and ran off to telephone their relatives the good news. Mona noticed someone else in the room, sitting in a chair against the wall, a paperback book in his hand. Above him hung a tilted sign.

Newt was holding her hand again. She looked up into his tired face and drifted off into a dreamless sleep.

A week passed, a quiet week of waking and sleeping and growing stronger. Each time Mona woke her father was there, holding her hand. And Fido was there, reading.

Mona smiled at her father and sat up in bed.

"Guess what day this is, princess," he said excitedly.

Mona had no idea of the day or the month.

"It's Founders' Day!" Sissie announced, bursting into the room. She hastily propped up the pillows behind Mona, who was sinking back into the bed. "And I have a big surprise for you. The parade has been rerouted so it will pass right under your window."

Mona groaned a feeble protest.

"Same old Mona," Fido said, as the door flew open. Romulus and Remus, in identical uniforms, jogged in.

"We are the very model of a modern Major-General,
We've information vegetable, animal, and mineral. . . ."

"Just a little preview of what's to come," Romulus said, giving his niece a warm hug. Remus was still singing:

"I'm very well acquainted, too,
     with matters mathematical.
I understand equations,
     both the simple and quadratical. . . ."

"Oof!" The mathematical twin was knocked to the floor by a howling Great Dane.

"Mona, poochy," Kadota pounced on Mona and gave her a big wet kiss on her cheek, followed by nine Kanines with extended paws. Mona shook hands, and looked around the room. "Gracie Jo's getting dressed for the parade," Kadota explained, but that was not who Mona was looking for.

"Where's Uncle Truman?"

"He's been in an accident, princess," Newt explained, "but he's doing just fine: just two broken legs and a smashed elbow. He's in traction in the room under this one; that's how come your mother was allowed to tap-dance by your bed."

Mona now understood why the welcome-home sign was so crudely drawn. He must have made it in his hospital bed with one hand. "What kind of accident?"

Kadota explained. "Truman tied himself into such a tight knot that he rolled down the stairs. He couldn't call for help because his mouth was in his armpit. He had the crazy notion that he could find you in Capri and bring you home."

"What's so crazy about that?" Remus asked, brushing dog hairs from his major-general's uniform. "I thought the same myself. I divided and divided trying to reach zero, trying to reach you in Capri, Mona. My last fraction was so long I had to tape two rolls of toilet paper together to write it down."

"Were you really in Capri, Mona?" Fido asked.

Caprichos, Mona thought and wondered as Sissie shoved chattering people and yelping dogs out of the room. "Let's go, everybody; we've only got fifteen minutes before the parade begins. Come on, Newt honey."

Newt was still sitting at her bedside, holding his daughter's hand. "I'll stay here with Mona," he said.

Sissie stood alone at the door, staring back at the tender father-daughter scene. Mona looked up and saw the confused expression on her mother's face, an expression of hurt surprise, perhaps even jealousy.

"Go ahead, Newt," Mona said. "I'll be all right."

"But someone's got to stay with you, princess."

"I'll stay," Fido said.

2. FIDO'S DISEASE

FIDO STILL WORE his hangdog expression, but something was different about him. Mona didn't know what.

"Mona, I've got to ask you about. . . ." Fido's question was interrupted by Dr. Davenport.

"You look a bit pale, young lady," the doctor observed, feeling her pulse.

"Too much excitement," Mona tried to say around the thermometer in her mouth.

"Fine. You're doing just fine," he pronounced, completing his hasty checkup. "I want you to sit by that window and watch the parade; it will cheer you up. Best medicine there is, a parade. Got to run now and help my wife Sophie paste flowers on the big float. I'll look in on you later this evening. And I'll see you tomorrow, Fido, for another shot."

Fido blushed as the doctor scurried out of the room.

"I knew it, I knew it," Mona cried in disgust. "You get out of my room this minute, Fido Figg II, and take your venereal disease with you."

"It's not that, Mona, really it isn't," Fido protested. "It's just—just allergy shots."

Mona, about to sneer at the lame excuse, suddenly recognized the change in Fido: his nose wasn't running anymore. "What are you allergic to?" she asked dubiously.

"I can't tell you. I don't want anybody to know, especially my folks. Besides, you'll laugh."

"Try me," Mona challenged.

Fido hung his head and stuttered out his sad confession. "I'm allergic to d-d-dogs."

"Dogs!" Mona exclaimed, but she didn't laugh. Fido looked too pitiful for ridicule. "I won't tell anybody, I promise," Mona said.

Fido nodded gratefully, but something other than the absurd irony of his affliction seemed to be gnawing at him. "Mona, I've got to ask you something," he said hoarsely. "Mona, were you really in Capri?"

Mona remained silent, unwilling to reveal her secret, even to her troubled cousin. Besides, she was not sure there was a Caprichos; it could have been a feverish delusion, or a dream. *Her* dream.

"Please tell me, Mona," he begged pathetically. "I don't want to go there, but I've got to know. Did Uncle Florence want to go to Capri, or—or was he killed by the paint fumes?" Fido clutched the bedstead and seemed about to collapse under the burden of his terrible guilt.

"I was there, Fido," Mona said. "I was in Capri with Uncle Florence. And I've never seen him so happy. Phoebe was there, too. And just before I left, Uncle Florence said I must remember to thank you for his wonderful birthday present."

"Really?"

"Really," Mona said firmly. "Now go and join the parade."

Fido yelped with joy, ran out of the door, ran in again to kiss her on the forehead, ran out again, and ran in once more with another question. "Mona, how much does a first edition of *Lord Jim* cost?"

"One hundred dollars. But I'll let you have it for seventy-five, in installments." Mona smiled as her first customer ran out the door to join the marchers. Then slowly she climbed down from the bed. She was going to watch the parade.

★ ★ ★ ★ ★

3. PARADE WATCHING

★ ★ ★ ★ ★

FIGGS!" hissed Mrs. Lumpholtz.

Mona stood motionless in the middle of the room, her shoulders rigid. She almost wished she were back in the jungle with the creeping, crawling snakes.

"Mona Lisa Newton, you're a Figg through and through. Just look at you running around in bare feet, and your being so sick. Here, take this!" Mrs. Lumpholtz handed Mona a wrapped shoebox.

A drum ruffled; a sour trumpet heralded the start of the Founders' Day parade.

"Open it up, for heaven's sakes. I made them for poor Florence, but he won't be needing them anymore, God rest his kind soul. Here, let me help you." Alma Lumpholtz led the trembling patient to the window seat and unwrapped her gift. What Mona had once thought a bomb was a pair of crocheted slippers.

"See, a perfect fit," Mrs. Lumpholtz said, placing them on Mona's cold feet.

A whine of bagpipes proclaimed that the sanitation department was doing its fling.

"Thank you, Mrs. Lumpholtz," Mona said. "Would you like to watch the parade from my window?"

"Don't mind if I do." Mrs. Lumpholtz dragged a chair to the window as another visitor entered the room.

The girl scouts, dressed as pine cones, and their mothers, waving crab-apple blossoms, danced by.

"Hello, Mona, you're certainly looking better than you did the last time I saw you," the librarian said. "I thought you might like this book."

"Thanks, Miss Quigley." Mona was delighted with

the gift, *The Amenities of Book Collecting,* and even more delighted that the librarian was not angry with her. "How come you're not in the parade?"

"Careful, Mona," Miss Quigley replied in a pretended huff. "I forgave you once, when I learned you were only asking for a Conrad title, but if you are going to tell me that I have a natural musical talent and should be down there strutting to 'Bye, Bye Blackbird' I'll never lend you another book."

"I didn't mean that, really, Miss Quigley," Mona said.

"Well, I'll forgive you if you let me watch the folks making fools of themselves from your window."

Mona didn't know whether or not to take Miss Quigley seriously.

"Make yourself at home, Rebecca," Mrs. Lumpholtz said, moving her chair aside to make room for the librarian.

★ ★ ★ ★ ★

Bump Popham rode by in the sky-blue Studebaker followed by the tap-dancing Pineapple Slicers, carrying the star pitcher on their shoulders. Fido, still clutching his Joseph Conrad paperback, waved cheerfully up at Mona. He sneezed. Behind him Kadota led the performing Kanines, who stood on their hind legs and shook paws with one another.

★ ★ ★ ★ ★

Mona laughed heartily and Mrs. Lumpholtz and Miss Quigley applauded the perfect performance.

A papier-mâché Grubb Hill rumbled into view. On its pinnacle, dressed in pioneer buckskin, stood Gracie Jo, her eyes shaded with one hand, the other pointing to an imagined new town. At her side, also pointing, was a bird dog. Gracie Jo's imitation of a statue was so convincing that two pigeons came to roost on her head. Behind the float trotted an impromptu cortege of six stray dogs, a hog, two goats, and Noodles.

★ ★ ★ ★ ★

"Noodles!" Mona leaned out of her window and called to her runaway cat. Noodles looked up at the window and darted into the hospital so quickly that by the time the raspberry-red Edsel hove into sight the cat was purring in Mona's lap.

★ ★ ★ ★ ★

"We are the very models of a modern Major-General. . . ." Romulus and Remus performed their act on the roof of the car.

★ ★ ★ ★ ★

"Bravo!" Mona shouted. Mrs. Lumpholtz and Miss Quigley stood up to applaud the twins.

"I wish Uncle Truman were watching with us," Mona said, reading her sign for the hundredth time.

"Don't worry about Truman, he's doing just fine," Mrs. Lumpholtz said. "Harriet Kluttz hasn't left his side since the accident."

"An ideal couple," Miss Quigley said, and Mona decided she approved the romance.

The volunteer fire department's sirens blared.

"Excuse me, may I come in?"

Mona uttered a surprised gasp as the tall, birdlike man tottered into the room. She had thought Ebenezer Bargain was dead.

★ ★ ★ ★ ★

4. SAINTS GO MARCHING IN

★ ★ ★ ★ ★

SIT DOWN and join us, Eb," Miss Quigley said to the old bookseller.

"No, thank you, I just dropped by to give Mona some books."

"Look, look," Mrs. Lumpholtz shrieked. "There goes my little granddaughter."

★ ★ ★ ★ ★

Thirty kindergarten children, dressed as Pineapple lollipops, sang and danced under the window.

★ ★ ★ ★ ★

Everyone looked and told Mrs. Lumpholtz that her granddaughter did, indeed, look like a Pineapple lollipop.

Mr. Bargain placed a book in Mona's hand.

Mona didn't recognize the slim volume cased in new leather. She opened it to the title page:

THE
FIGG-NEWTON
GIANT

BY

Mona Lisa Newton

THE BARGAIN PRESS
Pineapple

"Look at the colophon," the bookseller said.

Mona turned the pages of her printed composition to the back of the book.

DESIGNED AND PRINTED BY EBENEZER BARGAIN

AT THE BARGAIN PRESS

IN AN EDITION OF TWO COPIES OF WHICH

THIS IS NUMBER *1*

"I'd/like to keep the second copy to remind me of my dear friend Florence Figg. I miss him so much."

Mona admired the beautifully made book in her hand. Her book, her words, her creation. She looked up gratefully to thank the old man, but he was bent over, pulling another book out of his briefcase. Mona stared at the familiar bald spot on the top of his head.

And then she knew.

★ ★ ★ ★ ★

The Horticultural Society, led by Sophie Davenport, tiptoed through the tulips.

★ ★ ★ ★ ★

"This is for you, too, Mona," Ebenezer Bargain said, straightening up. "Florence traded this book to me for two Conrads, just before he died. He loved the book so, and he loved you so—well, I want you to have it now. I'm too old to retire, and who knows. . . ."

Mona took *Las Hazañas Fantásticas* from his hand. "You'll live forever, Mr. Bargain, reading, collecting, and selling books in your little shop."

"Thank you for the lovely thought," he said.

★ ★ ★ ★ ★

The Pineapple High School band blared and a hundred young voices sang:
      "Oh, when the saints go marching in,
            When the saints go marching in,

We'll be proud to be in that number
When the saints go marching in."

Noodles, critical of the off-key harmony, darted off Mona's lap and hid under the bed.

Mona watched the old bookseller hobble out of the room. She could never imagine him without his bald spot, not in a nightmare, not in a dream. He had been recreated in that other-time, other-world place by someone else, someone too short to have ever seen the top of Ebenezer Bargain's head. Mona had seen him in Uncle Florence's dream. She had been to Capri!

"Good-bye, Mr. Bargain," Mona called after him. "And thank you, thank you so very much."

★ ★ ★ ★ ★

"And when the new world is revealed,
When the new world is revealed. . . ."

Mona thought of Uncle Florence, but not with sadness. She remembered him dancing with gentle Phoebe. He had found love and contentment; he was happy now, and there was no room for her in his small world.

It was the larger dream, someone else's magnificent dream of dreams that she would return to some day. If she were allowed.

With trembling hands Mona opened the original edition of *Las Hazañas Fantásticas.* Even her untrained eye could tell the difference between the harsh ink of the facsimile and the delicate tints she now studied. She tenderly ran her finger over the map until it stopped under a tiny, irregularly shaped island.

"Caprichos," it said. And drawn on the island, their leaves entwined, were two palm trees—one coral, one pink.

"Look, Mona." Miss Quigley pointed to the passing parade.

★ ★ ★ ★ ★

Newt was merrily honking the horn from the driver's seat of the flower-bedecked spring-green bus. He wore the costume of the King of Hearts. From a gilt throne on top of the float, throwing kisses and roses to the admiring crowd, reigned Penelope the Pinochle Queen of Pineapple—Sissie.

★ ★ ★ ★ ★

"Hooray!" shouted Mrs. Lumpholtz and Miss Quigley.

"Hooray!" Mona shouted, waving to her beaming parents. She clutched the would-be pirate's book to her breast and stared long and hard at the gay float as it drove past the cheering people of Pineapple. Mona wanted to remember this happy scene forever.

Mona had a lot of remembering to do, a lot of living and learning and loving to do, before she left once more for Caprichos. Before she returned to *their* dream.

"REALLY NOW, TRUMAN," I SAID. "THAT'S GOING TOO FAR.
IT'S SUPPOSED TO SAY 'END,' NOT 'AND.'"
"I LIKE IT BETTER THIS WAY," HE REPLIED.
MAYBE HE'S RIGHT.

★ ★ ★ ★ ★
★ ★ ★
★

Ellen Raskin lived in many worlds: in the world of books, in the world of dreams, and in New York City, where she wrote and illustrated in an 1820 haunted house.

Ellen Raskin was born in Milwaukee, Wisconsin, and grew up during the Great Depression. She is the author of several other novels, including the Newbery Award–winning *The Westing Game*, the Newbery Honor–winning *Figgs & Phantoms*, and *The Tattooed Potato and other clues*. She also wrote and illustrated many picture books, and was an accomplished graphic artist. She designed dust jackets for dozens of books, including the first edition of Madeleine L'Engle's classic *A Wrinkle in Time*. Ms. Raskin died at the age of fifty-six on August 8, 1984, in New York City.

Ellen Raskin made the illustrations in this book. She also designed this book with the patient assistance of Riki Levinson and Susan Shapiro (who is not responsible for Truman Figg's misspellings).

The typefaces were chosen to reflect the content of the words, to point up the contrast of old books with vaudeville. The text was set in Janson, a beautiful seventeenth-century old-style face. The display type is the theatrical Playbill. Truman's signs are composed of Chisel, Playbill, and News Gothic. The ampersand is Garamond. This sign represents the word "and" and is derived from the Latin *et*, which also means "and."

Turn the page
to read the first chapter of Ellen Raskin's
Newbery Award–winning novel,

THE
WESTING
GAME

■ SUNSET TOWERS ■

1

THE SUN SETS in the west (just about everyone knows that), but Sunset Towers faced east. Strange!

Sunset Towers faced east and had no towers. This glittery, glassy apartment house stood alone on the Lake Michigan shore five stories high. Five empty stories high.

Then one day (it happened to be the Fourth of July), a most uncommon-looking delivery boy rode around town slipping letters under the doors of the chosen tenants-to-be. The letters were signed *Barney Northrup*.

The delivery boy was sixty-two years old, and there was no such person as Barney Northrup.

■ ■ ■ ■ ■ ■ ■ ■ ■ ■ ■ ■

Dear Lucky One:

Here it is—the apartment you've always dreamed of, at a
rent you can afford, in the newest, most luxurious building
on Lake Michigan:

SUNSET TOWERS

- Picture windows in every room
- Uniformed doorman, maid service
- Central air conditioning, hi-speed elevator
- Exclusive neighborhood, near excellent schools
- Etc., etc.

You have to see it to believe it. But these unbelievably elegant apartments will be shown by appointment only. So
hurry, there are only a few left!!! Call me now at 276-7474
for this once-in-a-lifetime offer.

Your servant,
Barney Northrup

P.S. I am also renting ideal space for:
- Doctor's office in lobby
- Coffee shop with entrance from parking lot
- Hi-class restaurant on entire top floor

■ ■ ■ ■ ■ ■ ■ ■ ■ ■ ■

Six letters were delivered, just six. Six appointments were made,
and one by one, family by family, talk, talk, talk, Barney Northrup led the tours around and about Sunset Towers.

"Take a look at all that glass. One-way glass," Barney Northrup said. "You can see out, nobody can see in."

Looking up, the Wexlers (the first appointment of the day)

were blinded by the blast of morning sun that flashed off the face of the building.

"See those chandeliers? Crystal!" Barney Northrup said, slicking his black moustache and straightening his hand-painted tie in the lobby's mirrored wall. "How about this carpeting? Three inches thick!"

"Gorgeous," Mrs. Wexler replied, clutching her husband's arm as her high heels wobbled in the deep plush pile. She, too, managed an approving glance in the mirror before the elevator door opened.

"You're really in luck," Barney Northrup said. "There's only one apartment left, but you'll love it. It was meant for you." He flung open the door to 3D. "Now, is that breathtaking, or is that breathtaking?"

Mrs. Wexler gasped; it was breathtaking, all right. Two walls of the living room were floor-to-ceiling glass. Following Barney Northrup's lead, she ooh-ed and aah-ed her joyous way through the entire apartment.

Her trailing husband was less enthusiastic. "What's this, a bedroom or a closet?" Jake Wexler asked, peering into the last room.

"It's a bedroom, of course," his wife replied.

"It looks like a closet."

"Oh Jake, this apartment is perfect for us, just perfect," Grace Wexler argued in a whining coo. The third bedroom was a trifle small, but it would do just fine for Turtle. "And think what it means having your office in the lobby, Jake; no more driving to and from work, no more mowing the lawn or shoveling snow."

"Let me remind you," Barney Northrup said, "the rent here is cheaper than what your old house costs in upkeep."

How would he know that, Jake wondered.

Grace stood before the front window where, beyond the road, beyond the trees, Lake Michigan lay calm and glistening. A lake view! Just wait until those so-called friends of hers with their classy houses see this place. The furniture would have to be reupholstered; no, she'd buy new furniture—beige velvet. And she'd have stationery made—blue with a deckle edge, her name and fancy address in swirling type across the top: *Grace Windsor Wexler, Sunset Towers on the Lake Shore.*

■ ■ ■ ■ ■ ■ ■ ■ ■ ■ ■

Not every tenant-to-be was quite as overjoyed as Grace Windsor Wexler. Arriving in the late afternoon, Sydelle Pulaski looked up and saw only the dim, warped reflections of treetops and drifting clouds in the glass face of Sunset Towers.

"You're really in luck," Barney Northrup said for the sixth and last time. "There's only one apartment left, but you'll love it. It was meant for you." He flung open the door to a one-bedroom apartment in the rear. "Now, is that breathtaking or is that breathtaking?"

"Not especially," Sydelle Pulaski replied as she blinked into the rays of the summer sun setting behind the parking lot. She had waited all these years for a place of her own, and here it was, in an elegant building where rich people lived. But she wanted a lake view.

"The front apartments are taken," Barney Northrup said. "Besides, the rent's too steep for a secretary's salary. Believe me, you get the same luxuries here at a third of the price."

At least the view from the side window was pleasant. "Are you sure nobody can see in?" Sydelle Pulaski asked.

"Absolutely," Barney Northrup said, following her suspicious stare to the mansion on the north cliff. "That's just the old Westing house up there; it hasn't been lived in for fifteen years."

"Well, I'll have to think it over."

"I have twenty people begging for this apartment," Barney Northrup said, lying through his buckteeth. "Take it or leave it."

"I'll take it."

Whoever, whatever else he was, Barney Northrup was a good salesman. In one day he had rented all of Sunset Towers to the

people whose names were already printed on the mailboxes in an
alcove off the lobby:

OFFICE ❑	*Dr. Wexler*
LOBBY ❑	*Theodorakis Coffee Shop*
2C ❑	*F. Baumbach*
2D ❑	*Theodorakis*
3C ❑	*S. Pulaski*
3D ❑	*Wexler*
4C ❑	*Hoo*
4D ❑	*J. J. Ford*
5 ❑	*Shin Hoo's Restaurant*

Who were these people, these specially selected tenants? They
were mothers and fathers and children. A dressmaker, a secretary,
an inventor, a doctor, a judge. And, oh yes, one was a bookie, one
was a burglar, one was a bomber, and one was a mistake. Barney
Northrup had rented one of the apartments to the wrong person.

Don't miss any of Ellen Raskin's
clever mysteries!

Hardcover 978-0-525-42369-0
Paperback 978-0-14-241700-3

Hardcover 978-0-525-42367-6
Paperback 978-0-14-241169-8

Hardcover 978-0-525-42368-3
Paperback 978-0-14-241699-0

Dutton 25th Anniversary Edition
978-0-525-47137-0

Puffin Premium Edition
978-0-14-038664-6

Puffin Modern Classics Edition
978-0-14-240120-0